CW01496124

Joan + Michael

Many thanks for your
hospitality

December 16/17 1992

" God bless us, every one "

Douglas Verrall

P.S. Darkness is cheap!

TWENTY STORIES

A South East Arts Collection

Edited by

Francis King

Published in association with South East Arts by

SECKER & WARBURG

LONDON

First published in England 1985 by
Martin Secker & Warburg Limited
54 Poland Street, London W1V 3DF
in association with
South East Arts
9–10 Crescent Road, Tunbridge Wells,
Kent TN1 2LU

Selection and Introduction © South East Arts 1985
Copyright remains with the individual contributors

"Kinderspiel" first appeared in *2 PLUS 2* and is reprinted with their
permission.

British Library Cataloguing in Publication Data

Twenty stories: a South East Arts collection.
1. Short stories, English   2. English fiction
—20th century
I. King, Francis, *1923*–   II. South East Arts
823'.01'08[FS]   PR1309.S5

ISBN 0-436-23385-1

Photoset in Linotron 202 Bembo 11/12 by
Rowland Phototypesetting Limited, Bury St Edmunds, Suffolk
and printed by St Edmundsbury Press
Bury St Edmunds, Suffolk

EDITOR'S INTRODUCTION

Many years ago I dropped in on my then publisher, Mark Longman, in his office. Having astutely twigged that writers, like dogs, need to be constantly stroked and patted in order to be happy, he at once gushed: 'Oh, I *did* so enjoy that last story of yours in *Encounter!*' I took a package from my brief-case: 'I'm so glad to hear that. I've brought you a collection of my stories.' This information made him look as stricken as if I had said: 'I've brought you some bacilli of the plague.'

What better confirmation could there be of the repeated assertion that the short-story, a literary form that reached maturity less than a hundred years ago, has already gone into a premature decline? Like Mark Longman, publishers usually bring out collections of short-stories only in order to encourage their authors to produce something else – 'something full-scale', as they often put it. People, we are constantly told, no longer read short-stories, now that many of the magazines – the *Argosy*, the *Strand* and *Blackwood's* at once come to mind – that used to publish them have vanished along with some of the railway lines on which they helped to while away the time. Literary editors let volumes of short-stories accumulate on their shelves and then, with a sigh, despatch them to some reviewer to receive the summary execution of a paragraph each. Writers like V. S. Pritchett, A. L. Barker, and Fred Urquhart (here represented) would be far more widely known to the reading public if the novel, and not the short-story, were the field in which they excelled.

Yet, obstinately, innumerable short-stories go on being written and, no less obstinately, some of those innumerable

short-stories go on being published and read. The area, com-
prising Kent, Surrey and East Sussex, served by South East
Arts is small, if highly populated. Who would imagine that the
submissions for a short-story collection from such an area
would run not into tens but into hundreds? And who would
imagine that the writers of those stories would span a whole
spectrum ranging from those clearly still at school to those no
less clearly writing out of their memories of the First World
War?

Many of these submissions came from obvious amateurs,
but amateurs in the sense not merely of non-professionals but
of lovers of the genre. Such submissions often took the form of
fragments of autobiography, rather than of short-stories,
consciously shaped, in the true sense. Though I felt them to be
unsuitable for a collection such as this, I nonetheless found
them fascinating – it was as though pieces of oral history had
been transcribed word for word at the moment of their
relation. I can do no more than guess if F. Bennett's *Dingo*,
included here, is fiction or reminiscence of such a kind; but I
should guess that, for all its artistic completeness, it falls into
the second of these categories.

Certain themes constantly recurred. One of these was the
relationship – explored in Philip Smith's *The Wedding Jug* and
Rosemary Sayers's *Mrs Llewellyn* – between the representa-
tives of widely separated generations. Another was the sort of
marriage that is beginning slowly and subtly to unravel, like a
knitted garment snagged on brambles or depredated by moth.
In their different ways, Clare West's *Life in the Sun*, Douglas
Verrall's *Behind a Stone* and Dick Kempson's *A Walk on the
Common* all make effective use of this theme. Curiously, there
were a number of submissions that took a funeral as a starting-
point – as do Rosemary Sayers's *Mrs Llewellyn* and Nicholas
Burbridge's *Digging for Gold* – but only one, rejected after long
deliberation, that so took a birth. Other popular themes not
represented here included visiting a dying relative or friend in
hospital; the experience of a nervous breakdown; and conflict
between teacher and pupils, boss and employees, or sibling
and sibling.

There are some well-known writers represented in my final
choice. As a schoolboy in the early days of the Second World
War, I wrote a fan-letter to Fred Urquhart after reading his

pungent novel of Scottish slum-life *Time Will Knit* and some of his short-stories in *Encounter*. Since, after all these years, my enthusiasm for his work remains with me, I am happy to have been able to include his *Kinderspiel*, and indeed to award it the Barbara Campion Memorial Prize. Less well-known as a short-story writer than as a novelist, Thomas Hinde has contributed his psychologically acute *Trust Mother Audry*. Among younger authors, I welcome contributions from Gabriel Josipovici (*The Bitter End*) and, ever effervescent, Wendy Perriam (*Angelfish*).

I should guess that some of the now unfamiliar names here included will soon become familiar. Of these, my own favourite is Kelvin I. Jones, whose *Mab's Hill* piquantly suggests the apprentice work of a modern M. R. James. Other readers will no doubt find favourites of their own.

The message of the whole collection is, I think, clear: Mark Twain's comment on his rumoured demise can be applied to the rumoured demise of the short-story – 'the report . . . was an exaggeration'.

August 1984   FRANCIS KING

The Bitter End

Gabriel Josipovici

Interviewer: '*Do you like to compose?*'
Stravinsky: '*Do you like to wake up*
in the morning?'

He is walking in a wood. It is early autumn but the leaves are already turning yellow and lying thickly on the ground. His mother comes towards him. He knows, though he couldn't say why, that she has come from the house, has come to meet him. She picks him up. He can feel her heart beating in her breast, under the ample folds of her dress. Her arms are warm round him. A tear falls on his face. It is hot and heavy, like oil.

He wakes up. Here he is high up above the city. The windows are closed. There is no sound. He draws a hand out from under the covers and touches his cheek.

The nurse comes in. 'We're awake now, are we?' she says. She goes to the window. Lets in light.

'How are we this morning?' she says.

She bustles about the room. Looms over the bed. 'We're looking well this morning,' she says.

The room. He has never minded what sort of room he had to work in. He has always prided himself on being able to work anywhere, under any conditions.

O. sits by the bed. She holds his hand in hers.

'It can't be done,' she says. 'They don't know what it means. That's why they have air-conditioning.'

'Take me somewhere else then. Where they open.'

'Windows just don't open in New York,' she says.

'Take me somewhere else.'

'Don't be silly,' she says. 'You know it's best for you here.'

'I feel I'm dead already,' he says. 'In this room up above the city with its sound-proof walls and its air-conditioning.' But perhaps he only thinks it, because she does not move, or reply, keeps his hand in hers and looks round for an ashtray as she is always doing. He has not known her without a cigarette in her hand and hunting for an ashtray.

The room is in darkness. His eyes have always been good but he cannot penetrate this darkness. He closes his eyes.

The pattern has not gone away.

O. holds his hand. The sun shines into the room. She holds his hand, sitting quite still beside the bed.

'He seemed better,' the nurse says. 'Yesterday he seemed better.'

O. will not talk about him to her. He feels her hand tensing round his.

'They're up and down an awful lot of course at that age,' the nurse says.

'We want to go away from here,' O. says. 'We want to go where you can open the windows.'

'You can't be better looked after than here,' the nurse says. 'New York has the best medical facilities in the world.'

'But the windows don't open,' O. says.

'The windows?'

'You know,' O. says. She makes a gesture with her free hand. 'Air. Wind.'

'The air-conditioning wouldn't work if you opened the windows,' the nurse says. 'Anyway, it's more hygienic like this.'

'How did people do in the old days?' O. asks.

'They died,' the nurse says.

'They die now,' O. says.

The pattern. Nine. He can feel the hum. One and nine and two and eight and three and seven and four and six and then five like a springboard at the centre. But that too is divided into nine. Nine small sections. And the fifth of these small sections sub-divides again, it is turning very fast, whirling, he touches it with his hand, just touches and lets the edges brush the palm, tickle the palm.

The nurse pulls up the blinds. She turns: 'How are we this morning?'

He holds his hand out to her.

'What is it? What do you want to show me?'

It whirls. It strokes the palm, it tickles the base of the fingers. 'What?' she says. She holds up the hand. There are two sets of sensations then, quite distinct: her hand, holding his at the wrist; and the last vestiges of the whirling, the stroking, the tickling.

'What are you trying to show me?' she says.

She holds his hand up to the light. She lays it back on his chest.

'You look good this morning,' she says. 'I just hope I look half so good at eighty-five.'

O.

Her hand over his.

'Ah,' he says.

She takes the cigarette out of her mouth and puts it between his lips. He puffs quickly and she removes it. He squeezes her hand.

His father is standing at the end of the terrace. He is talking to another man. He gestures at him to come and join them. He starts to walk along the terrace towards them.

The two men have stopped talking. They are standing very close to each other, watching him approach.

He is walking along the terrace towards them. Beyond the terrace, on his right, is the lawn, and then the woods start. He can hear his shoes creaking as he walks. He can feel the cold stone of the terrace through the thin soles.

The word nasturtium.

A little train at the seaside, running along the beach. The word nasturtium.

The little hills. The valleys. Into the tunnel. Into the bend of the Ess.

'Soon we'll have you back on your feet,' the nurse says. Her name is Elena. 'Call me Elena,' she says.

'I knew an Elena,' he says. 'I was in love with an Elena once.'

'You don't say?'

'She was like you too, in some ways.'

'You're teasing me.'

'My teasing days are over,' he says.

'Oh come on! We'll have you back on your feet in no time.'

'My feet,' he says. 'I doubt if they will ever want to have much to do with me again.'

The dark. Behind the word. In the little train. The sea on

one side, the houses of the promenade on the other. A voice says: 'It is the back of nasturtium.'

And another pattern. Two quite separate stories. And then one is seen to be the back of the other. The back of nasturtium. The other reversed. So that they are no longer two. Yet not one. The train chugs. It fills with children. Nasty. Tertius. Tertium. Tershum. A nasty cold. A nasal ort.

But why the train?

'What train?' O. asks.

'Train?'

She squeezes his hand.

'I smelled his breath,' the nurse says. 'You gave him a puff.'

'You begrudge him that?'

'You heard what the doctor said,' the nurse says. 'You want him to get well or you want to kill him?'

'I want him to be happy.'

The terrace. His father looks down at his shoes.

'I don't know why I was always frightened of Mother,' he says to O.

'I wasn't frightened of her,' O. says.

'I know.'

O. stubs out her cigarette in the ashtray on the little table beside her. She is smiling a little, to herself.

'It's him I should have been frightened of, not her.'

He puts his hand up to his cheek at the memory of the tear, and then there is the pattern again. Nine. And eight and two *outside* one and nine. And seven and three *outside* eight and two. And six and four *outside* seven and three. And round the periphery, over the whole spherical surface, for it has become a sphere now, the five, the nine times nine times nine times nine elements of five.

The terrace. The house. The woods. Autumn leaves.

'Why do your shoes creak like that?' his father asks.

No.

Why these images? Why them and not others?

His father stands and talks to a visitor. He watches from the other end of the terrace.

Her arms round him. He buries his face in the warmth of her dress.

The house. The terrace. The curtain comes down. The audience claps.

O.

'The doctor asked me not to smoke in here any more.'

'You said he said you could.'

'Now he's asked me not to.'

'Ignore him.'

'No. I can't.'

It frightens him that she accepts the doctor's ruling. She has never stopped smoking for anyone. She senses his fear and holds his hand more tightly.

'We'll change doctors.'

'No,' she says.

He thinks: she could have gone on smoking so as not to frighten me. That she chooses to frighten me means that she feels there is hope. But there is no hope. She wants to give me hope even at the cost of frightening me. But there is no hope. She knows there is no hope and I know there is no hope. But then why has she stopped?

She has never felt the need to question his silences. To ask. There have never been any lies between them. Not where it matters.

How many little lies? How many unimportant lies?

So it is a play.

Now the curtain is up and the verandah and the house are visible again. Perhaps there are two curtains. Two plays. A play within a play. But the second play is identical to the first. The set is the same. The characters are the same. The dialogue, after a pause, continues in the same vein.

The characters step from the one stage into the second. And then go on with the same play. And when the audience is accustomed to it once more, the second set is also revealed as only a set. .

What a bore.

His body has shrunk under the covers. He is so small he hardly raises a lump on the bed.

'We'll soon have you on your toes again,' the nurse says.

'I have never walked on my toes.'

'Oh?'

'Have you?'

'What?'

'Ever walked on your toes?'

'I can't say I have,' she says. She sits him up, helps him to eat. 'There's a good boy,' she says.

'Nurse,' he says, 'I am eighty-five years old. Your command of the English language must be somewhat defective if you imagine that a man of eighty-five should be called a boy.'

'Defective?' she says. 'Did say defective?'

'Nurse,' he says, 'do I have to speak to you in words of one syllable?'

'Oh, I know what defective means.'

'You do?'

'Yeah. Sure. I was just surprised to hear you using the word.'

'Why should my using it surprise you?'

'I don't know. It just did.'

'Does my vocabulary generally surprise you?'

'There,' she says. 'You've eaten it all. We'll have you back on your feet in no time.'

'And what use would that be?'

'Use?' she repeats, surprised.

'All my life,' he says to her, 'I have dreamed about my work, and then when I have woken up I have gone to my desk and worked until I had got it down.'

'Oh yes?'

'That doesn't happen any more.'

'You don't dream?'

'Yes, I dream. I can't recompose it in words any more.'

'Why not?'

'I lack the will.'

'You could give it a try,' she says.

'Nurse,' he says. 'I have never *tried* in my life. I have either done something or I haven't. I don't know what it means to *try* to write.'

She is silent. Then she says: 'Why don't you write then?'

'I told you. I lack the will.'

'Perhaps for the moment you do,' she says. 'You'll see. It'll come back.'

'I cannot remember a time when I lacked it,' he says. 'In all my eighty-five years I cannot remember such a time. It is finished.'

'Don't say that,' she says. 'You'll write plenty of beautiful things yet.'

'Plenty,' he says. 'Of beautiful things. Yet.'

Why did the shoes creak? Were they new? Did they always creak? Or is it only in the memory?

'We were wondering,' his father says as he comes up to them, 'if you could tell us what the new rules are in the game of tennis?'

The doctor. 'I forbid you to smoke in this room. I categorically forbid it.'

Her fingers. 'Look at my fingers,' she says. 'I promised my mother I would never have nicotine-stained fingers.'

She holds her hand up to the light. 'I promised her that if I had to smoke I would always use a holder. She didn't want me to smoke but she knew we cannot always do what we should. She was aware of the virtues of compromise.'

A movement forward. Into itself. It starts. It moves inexorably forward. It arrives – at the start.

The dark. The silence.

He is walking forward. He is entering a room. He has been in this room before. When?

The dark. The silence.

The furniture in the room. The photos on the mantelpiece. He has been in this room before.

The photos. A man in uniform with a moustache. A woman with a dog.

The windows are closed. There is dust on the mantelpiece. He runs his finger along the mantelpiece through the dust. It leaves no trace.

The window. He looks through the window at the garden beyond.

He comes back to the photos. He picks up the photo of the woman with the dog. Turns it over. There is writing on the other side.

He cannot read the writing. He cannot decipher the words. He cannot make sense of the letters.

O.

She puts her hand on his, through the covers.

The room. The dust on the little round table by the window. He stretches out his hand.

Forward. One step leading to another. Till at last you are back at the beginning. But not a circle. A straight line. Straight forward into the beginning.

He says to O.: 'I was so frightened of Mother all my life. And now she comes to me in my dreams as the incarnation of love.'

O. says 'Not all your life. You have forgotten. It was only because of me that you were frightened of her.'

'She loved you.'

'You were frightened of her because of me.'

'My father was the one I loved. And now I am ashamed because my shoes creak as I walk towards him.'

O. presses his hand through the covers.

'What nonsense it all is,' he says.

'Why nonsense?'

'I want,' he says. 'Oh I want.'

'What?' she says. But she knows. She presses his hand.

The nurse indicates that it is time for her to go. They stand by the window and talk.

'Open the window,' he says to O. 'Tell her to open the window.'

They do not respond.

'Tell her to open the window.'

O. comes back to the bed. 'If you want,' she says, 'we can leave here tomorrow. We can find a place where the windows will open.'

'It doesn't matter.'

'If you want.'

'It doesn't matter.'

Read it one way, it's one story. Read it another, it's another. First it's about him. A man dying. Then it's about me. I cannot speak. Not openly. If I speak it will be something else. Not this. It will no longer be about the failure of the will to live, about the final refusal to speak. So it has to be about him.

The dark. The silence.

It is always a question of finding the limits. Of liberating the possibilities of the subject. When that is found it becomes possible to do it.

The nurse.

'You know how I used to know a book was really there? Really going to get written?'

'I met someone who admires your work. A friend of my brother's. He was really excited to learn that I was looking after you.'

'I would have a sense of the book. The finished object. Of the physical presence of it. I would dream it was there on the table in front of me. I would open it and the title would be there. And under it my name.'

'He asked me if I'd ask you to sign a copy of one of your books for him, if I brought it to you.'

'And I'd turn the page, to see how it started, but I couldn't. However much I tried I couldn't. But I knew it was there. It was all there. All printed.'

'Would you do that do you think?'

'I had to get down to work then. That was how I knew I had to get down to work. I couldn't just turn the page. I had to make those pages come into being.'

'Would you?'

'Like tracing words that were very pale. Sometimes they were invisible. But I knew they were there. It was not that the page was blank. It was all there, but invisible. So I had to make them visible. It wasn't easy. But no matter what the obstacles I knew I would get there in the end. I had to, you see. The book was already there. It was already written. I just had to help it become visible.'

'If I brought you a copy, would you?'

'Yes. Of course I would. For you.'

'I'll tell him. He'll be thrilled.'

'Now I can't work I don't want to dream any more.'

'He really will. I'll tell him. I'll tell him tomorrow.'

'Why should I go on dreaming if I can't get up and set to work any more? Why?'

'Perhaps,' she says, 'if we propped you up you could try one or two mornings, couldn't you?'

'I told you,' he says, 'it's not a question of trying. Do I have to repeat everything I say to you?'

'I'm sorry.'

'It doesn't matter.'

'Can't you will yourself to will?'

'No.'

'Don't say that,' she says.

'Why can't it all finish?' he says. 'Why can't it all be finished?'

'You're not to speak like that!' she says.

'What pains me, you see,' he says, 'is still imagining. Still hearing in my head. Still seeing in my head. Still feeling the form trying to emerge. And then I can't do anything about it.'

'You're weak yet. Give yourself a chance.'

'Yes,' he says.

He lies on the bed. His body is so tiny it hardly raises the covers. He waits for her to finish and go away.

Silence. Darkness.

The patterns. They quiver, buzz. He knows that he must not stir or they will vanish. Though they only torment him now he cannot let them go. Yet, even so, though he is so still he is hardly breathing, they disappear. Trickle away.

O.

He has no need to say to her: You made everything possible.

She holds his hand. He does not feel it, only sees that his hand is lying on the cover and hers is over it.

She knows what he is thinking.

She knows that he is right not to hope any longer. She knows that he has always known with absolute sureness when something had to be started, when it was finished.

Of course there are moments of rebellion. Moments filled with impossible fancies. Moments when he cannot believe it is all coming to an end, here, in this room, with so little fuss.

It has never been a matter of inspiration. Only of clarity of mind allied to will. Now the will has gone it is time to stop. To let it all go.

He does not want to go on. Not as he is. He does not want to speak to them any more. Not to any of them. Not even, he realizes with a kind of distant astonishment, to O. He has done with words.

For a moment he toys with the thought of that too as a pattern, and recalls the doubleness of that story, of the 'he' and the 'I' of that story, and then he lets it go.

I cannot speak the end of speech.

He watches with detachment as that pattern too slips away from him.

In his mind there is a very clear image: He stands on the quay, watching it go. Slowly, very slowly, he raises his hat and waves goodbye.

His body under the covers. He is so small now it is almost as though there was no-one there.

He does not move.

He is asleep.

The Holly Bears a Berry

Sylvia Monro

The Holly and the Ivy, now both are full well grown,
Of all the trees are in the wood the Holly bears the crown.

Piercing sweet, young voices rose through the cold air, as a band of children came swinging up the path from the valley.

'Danged little buggers. 'Nother quarter hour and I'd 'a been gone. Choir kids, I shouldn' wonder, getting it for the church. Likely they'll strip that last tree, and I could 'a used that.'

Pol Tilfer continued her soliloquy with pungent curses, but ceased when the children came within earshot.

O the rising of the sun, the running of the deer,
The playing of the merry organ, the singing of the choir.

The carol stopped as the party halted by the trees. One of the bigger boys spoke:

'Now then, you little ones can't reach to cut, so us big ones'll do that, and you collect up in bundles, and don't knock the berries off. Us cutters must be careful not to spoil the trees.'

The hollies were magnificent. Of the twenty or more, all richly dressed in glossy hunting green, most were flaunting a glory of scarlet berries which turned their tops to beacons, visible far and wide. Their skirts, bar one, bore only sparse red now, since much had been cut already.

The Commons Management Committee was wise enough to realize that holly berries are harder to preserve than a maiden's bloom. Birds take all that humans leave. And should picking be prohibited, the villagers, who counted this one of their traditional rights, would come surreptitiously, tearing

24

the branches off anyhow in their haste and anxiety not to get caught in the act.

So it was given out, in village hall and church and over the local grapevine, that there was plenty of holly up there on the hill for everyone, so long as each family took only enough for themselves. They were asked to cut carefully and not damage the trees, and at the same time to keep a good look out for 'poachers' who might try to steal the community heritage to sell for private profit. One season two men had come in a Landrover with a ladder and rope, and swiped the whole crop, leaving havoc in their wake. Recovery from their mutilations had taken years. Unfortunately the sole witness was a nervous creature, who fled as one might from murderers found finishing off a victim. By the time she reported it the culprits had vanished.

Pol Tilfer hadn't a Landrover, but she could tie an astonishing amount on to the ancient pram hidden in the wood behind the hollies. She was not a local inhabitant. She lived some miles away, but was sufficiently notorious to have earned the pseudonym of Pol Pilfer over a pretty wide area. She lived by her wits, and if her share of these was generous, it was the only thing about her that was.

She subsisted largely, and comfortably, off the land – albeit other people's land. Fruit, vegetables, eggs, poultry, flowers and even plants, indeed anything she could lay her thieving hands on, were all grist to her mill. What she didn't want herself she hawked from the pram in suitably distant places. An expert pick-pocket and shop-lifter, she was clever enough seldom to try the same trick too often. When, rarely, she was caught, her fines appeared to be less worry to her than to those who realized that any increase in her out-goings would inevitably be compensated by future intake.

Pol Pilfer hid in the wood, fuming silently, her mouth shut tight like a trap. Her shapeless brown coat was good camouflage. Often it was also good cover for countless pickings, but now the only thing it concealed, in a front pocket, was a very sharp knife with its point protected by a cork. All day people had come picking the holly. Whenever the coast was clear she had darted out and slashed off as much as possible, stacking it in dumps under the tall dead bracken.

Bloody hell, it would be dark soon. Looked as if it might

snow too. Cold as the grave it was. If only she'd left that last
tree and got the stuff on to the pram before the kids came. But
she hadn't. Garn, look at the price of holly in the shops.
Pounds and pounds and pounds worth she'd got, even at
hawking rates. She tried to reckon how much and her small
close-set eyes glinted. Would've been stupid not to suck the
orange dry. All the same, there'd be damn all to suck after
them kids . . . Gawd, it was getting dark fast, and colder.

At last the children left, singing again.

> *The holly bears a blossom as white as any flower,*
> *And Mary bore sweet Jesus Christ to be our sweet Saviour.*

Quick now. They'd not look back. Gather up the bundles.
Blimey, she was stiff from waiting. One pile, two, up to the
pram.

> *The holly bears a berry as red as any blood,*
> *And Mary bore sweet Jesus Christ to do poor sinners good.*

Three piles, four. Just the fifth left. Where was it? It was
hard to see in the undergrowth now. The singing was getting
distant, though still clear.

> *The holly bears a prickle as sharp as any thorn,*
> *And Mary bore sweet Jesus Christ on Christmas Day in the*
> *morn.*

Where the hell was that last pile? She stumbled over a hole in
the ground and lurched into a fallen trunk, catching her coat on
a jagged branch. The pocket ripped, and as she finally lost
balance, the knife slid sideways, cork dislodged. It fell frac-
tionally ahead of Pol herself, its heavy handle striking the
ground first, so that the point embedded itself in the inside of
her thigh.

If anyone heard her screech, which was unlikely, they
probably mistook it for that of a vixen making brazen love.
She rolled over involuntarily, wrenching out the blade in panic
agony, and tried to staunch the wound with pads of clothing.
But she'd never seen blood like this. Instead of welling out
gently, it spurted in uncontrollable jets of warm sticky horror.

As the snow began to fall, a dimness, other than the dusk, swirled in on her like a rising tide. Something was wrong with her eyes. Everything blurred. Only the children's voices still penetrated her terror and reached the dregs of consciousness. Piercing sweet, far and faint yet crystal clear as a thread of light from a door left ajar on a pitchy night.

> *The holly bears a bark as bitter as any gall,*
> *And Mary bore sweet Jesus Christ for to redeem us all!*

Then nothing. Only a swift-laid shroud of dazzling white, everywhere, except where a patch spread slowly, as red as any holly berry.

A Walk on the Common

Dick Kempson

The son was too big to be carried any distance, too small to walk far on his own. They had taken the bus in and there was no push-chair. The walk back across the Common had been a mistake. The week-end food was transferred from hand to hand with the same steady rhythm as the dusk falling. The two figures walked the path that divided the last sweep of the trees from the open space; the father, leant away from the heavy bag, making a protective arc over the slow progress of the boy. Without the sun the sky was luminous and strangely cold.

'Daddy. Daddy.'

The boy had stopped again, legs infirmly astride, face directed quizzically up at the figure of his father, tall as a tree. In his orange boots, orange romper suit and hood, with his old face, his father saw him as a foolish adult in fancy dress. The father waited, half turned, with a slow, mechanical patience.

'Daddy. They'll be closed in a minute. They'll be bloody closed, Daddy. Bloody closed. Bloody closed, Daddy.'

'Come on, son. D'you wanna pick-up?'

The boy remained where he was, silent, still watching his father. How strange, the man thought, that he should repeat that so long after it had been said – several hours now. But then the boy had developed this habit of imitating his parents, often in the most alarming ways. It was as if he contained everything and it grew with him. The father bent down and collected the boy who yielded passively.

They walked a hundred yards or so, the boy twisting uncomfortably in his father's grasp. He was put down and the

man looked hopelessly up the path ahead. How did she
struggle through the slow day and still have the energy to
fight? He looked away across the Common. A dog was
barking, a big brown dog leaping up at a woman, darting
across her path and coming round again. The woman walked
steadily on and the dog kept up with her in its teasing progress.

The boy was tottering onto the Common with his arms out
calling 'doggy'. He loved dogs, big, dangerous dogs that
studied his unpredictable advances warily. He knew no fear
with dogs. Something in them attracted him – their activity,
their games perhaps? It was hard to say.

'Simon. Simon, come back here. The doggy's too far away.
Simon.'

The boy ran on, twenty yards into the open ground, and
stood watching, seemingly oblivious to his father. The man
stood too for a moment, then in a frozen way stepped back
into the trees and was lost to sight.

The boy stood there, quite alone, in the great space of the
Common. He wasn't watching the dog anymore. He was
waiting for his father to sweep him upwards with angry
suddenness and then the tears of frustration and fatigue would
release him. But there was no-one coming behind him, no
long arm, no bristly face and breakfasty breath. He turned.
The long crowd of trees stared back. He turned full circle.
Where were the trees his father stood in front of? Had one half
of the world been swopped for something similar but with no
father? It was interesting. He turned. He laughed. He turned
again. Each time he expected his father to be behind him.
Perhaps his father was like a big, brown dog. They were
playing a game at last. But no, his father was not a big, brown
dog and there were only the remote, indistinguishable trees.
Perhaps his father was one of them. He ran forward a yard and
called 'Daddy'. He was too frightened to call loud and the big
space and the sky sucked the sound away in half a breath. Tears
came and in anger he called again, his cry taken away along the
laughing grass. His crying became howling, his hands went to
his face, palms across the eyes, and he was lost in weeping
amnesia.

Twenty yards into the trees the father crouched, watching.
He wanted to run to his son, catch him up high in his hands,
kiss his face and bury the sobbing in his hugging arms. But

something held him where he was, quite unable to move or speak. There were no thoughts; there was no pleasure in it. Because he had not made a decision to walk away he could not decide to go back. He was in a state of rigid fascination.

As the boy settled into a steady sitting and sobbing, the spell began to wear off. The father became conscious of the absurd, frightening situation. What was he doing? What unnatural cruelty lay within him? Was he simply to walk out there and continue as if the thing had never happened? Would the boy never forget? Would he tell her? A kind of depression settled on the man which made it easier to act without thinking. He stood stiffly, collected up the spilt bag and made his way across to the boy.

She sat with legs curled under, watching TV. She had on jeans and an old pink jersey with short sleeves that she did not like. She wore no make-up and her hair was pushed simply back following the perfunctory wash she had had when they left. The drink beside her had been absently refilled twice. She watched the quiz show with abstracted interest. It was always an amusing pastime with her to imagine the bitter rows the 'happy couples' fought but disguised for the sake of the show's image and their own greed. But no, of course, they were all probably perfectly happy in the sort of thoughtless way most people were. And all the time she thought this she wondered why they weren't home.

It was dark now. The boy would be exhausted. A simple chore – there, the shops and back again. And he would be slow and clumsily apologetic and a martyr to what he was doing for the family. Nothing angered her more than his softness. Nothing showed more clearly his misunderstanding and his inability to do anything about it. How attractive had been his careless assumption when they first met that he didn't need to think about what he did. But perhaps it had been easier then. Perhaps that kind of humour and game-playing could only be a short-term thing, thriving as it must have done on their not knowing each other and the tension of uncertainty. And now, of course, they knew everything there was to know and nothing was uncertain and gradually he had become stopped, immobile. What kind of games were there left to play?

The door chimed as the last happy contestants failed on the

car but carried away the fridge freezer, the teas-maid and the
£220. She made her way to the front door. From behind the
frosted glass two figures appeared as blurred shapes – one
small and close to the glass and the other behind, taller and less
distinct. She opened the door. There was a moment's pause
and then the boy hurried into his mother's legs and clung
there. The adults exchanged a look and then the woman
turned and walked into the house, pulling the boy from her
legs and stroking his head. The father watched them down the
hall, picked up the bag and carried it into the kitchen at the
back.

When he entered the living room they were sitting on the
floor in the middle of the room. He closed the door and went
behind the sofa. He stood there with his hands on the back of
it, watching. They had their backs to him – mother and child –
the boy curled into his mother with his head on her breast, her
hand stretched out onto the floor supporting his back, her chin
resting on his head. He was sobbing quietly and the mother
seemed to murmur back to him though she said nothing. The
man could not walk out from behind the sofa. He could not
cross the space and intrude. And when the boy's sobbing had
ceased and the woman carried him from the room he did not
look up or move. Only when he heard them upstairs in the
boy's bedroom did he walk across to the TV and switch it on.
It was a detective series – his favourite viewing. Men were
running through the trees. There were dogs. Someone had
found something – a coat. The men were looking at the coat
and each other. Someone would pay for this.

When he heard his wife come down the News was on and he
had finished her drink. She came in and stood behind him. He
turned. She stood there, her coat hanging from her hand. Her
lips were tight and pink and around her eyes a far-away
mountain blue. Her hair was combed out. She wore the dress
he liked to take her out in. It hugged the flanks at the tops of her
legs and cut across mid-way above the knee. She regarded him
and, twisted round, he looked up at her.

'Are we going out?'

'No. I am.'

'Where?'

She did not reply but walked out, leaving the living room

door open. He got up and followed her down the hall. At the front door he stopped her, a hand on her shoulder. She remained facing the door. Taking his hand away, he allowed it to brush down her back.

'When will you be back?'

'Later.'

If he hadn't given in, she might have relented. She pulled open the door and walked out. He followed her and stood at the end of their path. There was just grass at the front of their house, pavement, the road, pavement, more grass and the house opposite. Either way the wide road. She walked away slowly and disappeared over the rise. He stood there under the arc lamps in the big space between the houses. When she was gone he might have cried but instead he walked into the house.

He poured himself gin and tonic from a bottle bought that afternoon. He settled into the armchair with the TV playing aimlessly before him. It was a film made for TV with the ubiquitous sunshine colours and handsome actors. It was about a woman who had drifted into a small mid-Western town. All the men wanted to sleep with her but she was on the run for some reason and it was difficult to engage her interest for long. She seemed to promise them everything but the men were baffled by her strange depressions and her disappearances. Only one man on the outskirts of town who drank in the bars seemed to understand her. In the end he stopped drinking and she stopped drifting and the other men stopped trying to get her into bed and the woman and the man who had stopped drinking lived together on the outskirts of town.

He couldn't work out whether he was one of the men in the town or the one who lived on the outskirts. He wanted to be the man who could understand the woman but he suspected that he just wanted to get her into bed like all the rest.

He wondered where she was. He would like to meet her now as a stranger in some bar in town. He would not try to pick her up. He would be an intriguing character who did not have a house and a job like all the others. Finally, when they were drunk, they would go for a walk on the Common. She would walk with a sense of mystery wrapped about her and he would tease her with his dry wit. Inevitably, they would go to bed but neither would be able to predict the next day, ever.

She had walked down the hill to the junction at the bottom but avoided the local which they sometimes used. She walked to the other side of town. She was not intending to run away. She had brought no bags. She had no idea of a particular place to go. Eventually, the walking bored her and she went into a pub in the centre of town. It was crowded, noisy and smokey. Everyone seemed to be in large groups and ten years younger. She pulled herself onto the one remaining stool at the bar and waited to attract the barman's attention. He was probably her own age and big and smiling and when he pushed the drink towards her he did so as if he had bought it and she had not paid the generous price.

As she sat watching the people in the bar – young, flirtatious, irresponsible – she wondered if there might be some adventure here. The young boys with their protective girls? With the leering barman, who thought she was a tart? It was sordid. It was not an adventure. Adventures were not easily come-by, but perhaps adventures involved taking a chance. A gambler's fever consumes both the sordid and the beautiful. Were there safe adventures, board games played in living rooms through long evenings? Was life always its own adventure if you believed in the possibilities? She caught the barman's eye. She ordered another drink.

At one she returned. He was sitting in front of the empty screen. The evening's entertainment was long over but he had not switched off the buzzing that hummed inside his head, nor did he look round at her. She draped her coat over the chair and stroked his head. Then she bent down, her chin on his head, and stroked his chest. He reached up his hand and she held it. He began to sob and when, some time later, he was quiet, she took him upstairs to bed.

Mrs Llewellyn

Rosemary Sayers

P ine needles, fragrant, ubiquitous, martyrs to the central
heating, stipple packages beneath the branches. A square
parcel: it will be as it has been for the past twelve years, a tin of
assorted fancy biscuits. It is decorated with wax holly leaves,
saved from a pre-war Christmas cake. The card reads in
sloping copperplate: from Mrs Constance Llewellyn. No
bandying of christian names, no love, no season's greetings.
The card is attached with a neat strip of pink elastoplast, for
that was a house where no sellotape lay in the roll-top desk.
There was brown paper saved and folded and ironed, foul-
smelling sticky brown tape, and scratchy string from a tin
with a hole in the top; no fish fingers, no bought jam, no soft
lavatory paper, no heating in the bedrooms.

It is December 23 and I am going to her funeral. Like all
crematoria it is high on a hill. Scrubby standard roses line the
drive. Horizontal rain stabs in the wind across the car park.
There is a waiting room: no magazines, for we are not waiting
to have our teeth filled. Upright chairs are lined round the
small square room. I learn who I am: 'This is Mrs Dove, a
young friend of Mrs Llewellyn's – she used to live next door
when her children were small,' says Mrs Llewellyn's oldest
friend, Mr Murdoch, to his daughter Lesley Boakes from
Wales. She is older than I, and perhaps less presentable, being
plump. She wears a nylon fur coat and her skirt stops short
above her knees. Do not look at me like that, Lesley Boakes, I
am not a person who visits old ladies in order to be remembered in their wills. I am wearing my good (real, not cultured)

pearls and Gucci shoes to show you that my circumstances are
more than comfortable nowadays.

I never met Mr Llewellyn; he died the year before we moved
next door. His sister is here: eighty, short and fat in a plastic
mac and determined felt hat. Then there is Charlotte. I should
tell you that I believe in goodness. Charlotte is good. She is
also slow: slow, not stupid, slow, and small and now old.
Charlotte and Mrs Llewellyn loved each other. But was Mrs
Llewellyn also good?

The day we moved in was hell; no light bulbs, two children
then, tired and tearful, wanting only the familiar. I opened the
door to Charlotte, tiny in her green nylon overall and minnie-
mouse lace-ups. She bore a huge bunch of Mrs Simkins pinks.
They are white, actually: small-bloomed, frilled, easily deci-
mated by rain, short-lived once picked. I had never seen them
before. They had a heady, over-powering scent of cloves.
'Mrs Llewellyn from next door sent them to welcome the new
family,' chirruped Charlotte, and trotted back down the
path to the polishing of Indian brasses and the dusting of
corners.

Charlotte had come to Mrs Llewellyn when she was sixteen,
ten years younger than her employer; the fourteenth child of a
chalk quarryman, under-sized, illiterate, eyes slightly milky.
She came to the under-maid's attic bedroom, to the cleaning of
grates and washing up in the deep glazed sink surrounded by
its chintz skirt patterned with peacocks and improbable purple
pansies. She came to early mornings and hard work, and to
Mrs Llewellyn. She came to security, good meals, no more
beatings, praise for shining door knobs and well darned socks.
She came, and she stayed. She learned to read a little. She
learned not to be cheated on buses and in shops; to count the
change and her blessings. And when Mrs Llewellyn's father
died and she and Mr Llewellyn found the old house too big
without him, Charlotte went too to the bungalow where I
came to know them both.

I know all this because Mrs Llewellyn told me, bit by bit,
over the years. Dragging up that hill with push-chairs and
potatoes, I nearly always saw her, sitting by the window
beckoning in winter, and in spring and summer we talked over
the low garden wall. She was a gardener. I never knew her buy
a plant or seed – everything renewed itself, and most of the

stock in the little garden had come from what I too began to call the big house.

We are assembled, then, to say goodbye to Mrs Llewellyn. 'Sheep may safely graze' is coming from somewhere: there are likely-looking meshed vents high up in the wall. They cannot be part of some central heating system for the chapel is freezing. Lesley Boakes has ordered us according to her idea of precedence: she and Mr Murdoch in the front pew with Mrs Llewellyn's sister; behind them me, and a couple of other neighbours, and alone, behind us, Charlotte. The clergyman is obviously today's on-duty priest, bored. I look forward to the comfortable droning of familiar phrases. I shall think of Mrs Llewellyn in her greenhouse, arthritic, slow, fingering the twenty-five-year-old rat's tail cactus that hung over the door.

'. . . our sister, Mrs Constance Llewellyn,' says the priest, staring at a white fibre-glass urn of bronze plastic chrysanthemums. 'But I am sure you did not know her as Constance; Connie then, our sister Connie, whom we shall see no more on earth.' Hang on to the gothic arch of the pew in front. Do not scream that she was never Connie, who went to Bingo and was a senior citizen in fluffy bedroom slippers. She was Mrs Llewellyn, who cooked a proper lunch and laid the dining-room table every day of her life and murmured 'so kind' when a red-faced student nurse brought her tea in hospital. Even Mr Murdoch called her Mrs Llewellyn.

When I lived next door we shared the same window cleaner, Arthur Smallwood. We all called him Arthur, all of us in the road, except Mrs Llewellyn. He once asked her to. It would not be over-familiar, he said, not after seventeen years of cleaning her windows and discussing roses over a cup of tea afterwards. But she couldn't possibly, Mrs Llewellyn protested. 'When I see you coming up the hill with your bicycle and ladders and bucket, I think "Ah, good, Mr Smallwood is here,"' Mrs Llewellyn had replied. 'And Mr Smallwood you will always be.'

'. . . we shall all remember dear Connie in our own special ways, always remember, perhaps, things she said to us.'

I shall remember most what she didn't say. Mrs Llewellyn was all restraint, all good manners, all dignity. She glorified everyday clichés by their actual observance.

'We have to keep cheerful, don't we? Otherwise no-one will come to see me.' This when power cuts left her cold and frightened. The day they started, Charlotte arrived at our door clutching a parcel of candles. 'Frightening for the children in the dark, says Mrs Llewellyn.'

Mrs Llewellyn never came to our house, nor anywhere else. Her arthritis made it impossible. It was just as well, for, in our conversations, over the pelargoniums in summer, or at the chenille-covered table in winter, she somehow managed to build up a picture, unaided by me, of a Dove household run on smooth Edwardian lines. She had a day for every aspect of household cleaning. There they were then, Charlotte and Mrs Llewellyn, inured, secure, calm in their world of dusted door tops and rissoles on Mondays, each totally dependent on the other; safe in duty and thrift and ordered days.

The coffin is so small. Mrs Llewellyn was small; small and stout with ordered grey curls and red-veined cheeks. Lesley Boakes selected the flowers which lie on it: candy pink gerberas, a gaudy South African daisy. Mrs Llewellyn would not have liked them. She would have considered them vulgar. I should have chosen stephanotis, for she had that in her wedding bouquet, and scented white jasmine, and lilies: decorous, suitable. Aggressively new, with shiny brass handles, the coffin is gliding, but not noiselessly, through royal blue velvet curtains, supermarket conveyer belt to what Mrs Llewellyn would have called the great beyond.

I do not think she was especially religious, only in a conventional, well-behaved way. She simply never questioned the beliefs of her childhood. Was that the source of her strength then, never to question?

We sidle outside into the icy drizzle, and inspect the wreaths and sprays, limp in their damp cellophane. Lesley Boakes has sent by far the grandest. I chose mine, flower by flower. I asked one of the children to write the card. 'To Mrs Llewellyn, of whom we were all very fond', he put, in an unaccustomed burst of appropriately good grammar.

She liked him best, that last child. Perhaps it was because, like her, he was born long after his brother and sister.

Mrs Llewellyn had two sisters, gloriously named India and Mattie. They were ten and fifteen years older than she. I think they took advantage of her, although she never said so. She

told me how she handed them hairpins on the nights of balls
and parties, watching them climb into the cab, her nose
pressed against the window. When their mother died, the girls
had already left home and married, and Mrs Llewellyn stayed
at home to care for her ageing father, even after she and Vic
were married.

Her father had been very strict. On her fourteenth birthday
he had turned to her at dinner, when, as usual, she was eating
in silence. 'You are fourteen now, little Constance. Now you
may talk at table with the rest of us, but mind you have
something interesting to say, and never begin a conversation
with a question.'

Lesley Boakes enquires whether I have cleared the greenhouse. Apparently Mrs Llewellyn had wanted me to have her
plants. We made four journeys yesterday, filling the car with
cacti, over two hundred geranium cuttings, ferns and be-
gonias. Everything was in order; scrubbed flower pots stacked
beneath the bench, bucket for the dead leaves, meticulously
picked off daily. But when it was empty I turned, and saw that
the glass was mossy, and cracked in places, and the wooden
staging beginning to splinter. It was a sad place then, where we
had talked so often, Mrs Llewellyn with her deep throaty
laugh, waving her stick at some specimen in the back row.

Charlotte is standing alone, in a well-washed white mac, her
head covered by one of those ridiculous polythene triangles
secured by tapes beneath her chin. 'Where shall I go on
Wednesdays?' is all she says.

Two years ago Mrs Llewellyn and Charlotte were parted,
after nearly sixty years. Charlotte had to return to the little
terraced house of her sister, who needed nursing following a
stroke. Mrs Llewellyn engaged a daily woman, and only saw
Charlotte on Wednesdays, when she came for the day. Mrs
Llewellyn never told me how bereft she was. But she worried
about Charlotte: her seven stone had turned to six, for she had
never learned to cook well. Mrs Llewellyn had cooked lunch
each day, while Charlotte cleaned.

I had once called to find Mrs Llewellyn eating alone in the
dining room, while Charlotte sat at the kitchen table. I had
queried this feudal arrangement. 'Dear Charlotte, she
wouldn't be happy in here,' Mrs Llewellyn had replied.

For the past few years, since we moved, I saw less of Mrs

Llewellyn, and each time I saw that at last she was beginning to feel her eighty-five years. She never said so, of course. But she began to take a nap after lunch, before the washing up. She took longer to dress. My visits had to be planned now.

We used to sit in the dining-room, always on upright chairs. On a crocheted mat in the centre of the table was an Irisene – a tall plant with red leaves, grown on each year from cuttings originally raised by Mrs Llewellyn's father. Mrs Llewellyn smoked one of her two daily cigarettes, the red and gold du Maurier box behind her on the roll-top desk. As a rule we talked mostly of the past, although she always wanted to hear about the children, whose doings I censored and abridged before offering up for her approval. She led me into the soul of her past by way of absorbing trivia. She told me how at the big house, soap had come in a big block, which they had sawn up with a kitchen knife. She told me why all her generation had had their hair shingled. It had been a necessity forced on the girls who had become nurses during the first war – in order to prevent lice. When they had returned home shorn, the style had become the latest fashion. She told me how she had been the first girl in her class to possess her own piece of India rubber.

I asked how she was feeling, of course, and out came the clichés. She mustn't grumble, she had lots to be thankful for, the spring weather would cheer us all up.

Not me, I remember once thinking, pregnant with the last child. Mrs Llewellyn, while you worry about the price of wet fish and re-read *Cranford* and water your houseplants from the brass watering-can, I struggle with children and baked beans and washing. My husband comes home later and later each night. I am unhappy, Mrs Llewellyn. All is not well. There is no contented order to my life.

But I said that yes, spring and the delft blue hyacinths would brighten things up.

'And your dear children of course, Mrs Dove,' said Mrs Llewellyn. 'Lovely children.' And of course, they were. She and Vic had married too late for there to be babies. I knew she minded this a great deal, but she never said so. I wonder now if she knew what I never said to her. Perhaps.

Winter came late this year. There were buds on the Queen Elizabeth roses well into November, and Mrs Llewellyn lit only one of the two paraffin stoves in the greenhouse. She had a cough which never seemed to go away. One Wednesday, Charlotte phoned: she had never liked telephoning, and always shouted, holding the receiver well away from her mouth. Mrs Llewellyn had pleurisy. She had been taken to hospital and Charlotte had been asked to tell her friends. Arrangements had been made for Charlotte's sister, so that she could come and stay in the bungalow while it was empty.

The hospital, an old workhouse, was high on a hill on the edge of the town. Mrs Llewellyn was at the far end of the long ward, sitting up, pink and scrubbed in a pale blue flannel nightdress. The nurses were kind, the food was acceptable given the problems of mass catering, she was feeling better and soon expected to be home again. She mustn't grumble, she would have to make the best of it, but of course, everyone liked to be at home. She gave no indication of expecting anything other than a full recovery, and a resumption of life as it had always been.

And certainly, she looked well enough; vulnerable perhaps, but bed always does that to people. I asked her what the doctors had said. Not much. 'They tend to treat us as old sillies,' she said. But of course, she was not silly. On the table over the bed was her battered crocodile handbag. She fingered it with her purple, swollen hands from time to time, I fancied because it was comfortingly familiar. I promised to see that Charlotte was looking after the greenhouse.

She came home after a fortnight, and Charlotte stayed on. I called one evening, at Mrs Llewellyn's request. She wanted to see me before Christmas, she said. That would be the biscuits. They were in the dining-room, she and Charlotte. She sat, looking smaller, it seemed, on an upright chair at the table. She was fully dressed. The room was warm and bright, and Charlotte sat, neat in a hand-knitted apricot jersey, beside the fire. 'You do look a little tired,' I said to Mrs Llewellyn. It was only to be expected, she said. She would soon be her old self again. I went to help Charlotte with the tea. 'She stayed up all night,' Charlotte whispered over the tea caddy, 'because of the sheets. Her arthritis is so much worse that she can't get to the bathroom in time. She had an accident the first night home, and now she won't go to bed, she just sits up in the chair.'

I did not know what to say. We watch the legs of strange

women parted to give birth, the cutting of the dead white cord, watch soldiers dead on burnt grass, their maroon blood dry on khaki shirts, watch the glistening pumping chests of men making love in second-rate plays, listen to studio discussions on cancer, the testimonies of women without breasts. But I did not know what to say to Mrs Llewellyn who was afraid of wetting her bed.

I told Charlotte she must make her go to bed, tell her that the washing of sheets was unimportant. I told Mrs Llewellyn she must have a good night's sleep. That was all. I should like to have kissed her when I left; I do not know why. I didn't of course, for that would have been breaking the rules. It would have acknowledged how fond we were of each other. I merely said I would call over Christmas, and she said that would be lovely and sent her love to the children, and a one pound coin for each of them.

Charlotte phoned the next morning to say that she had died in her sleep, in bed, where she had agreed to go.

'What a blessing. She was cheerful to the last,' says Lesley Boakes, whose charmless clichés are without the integrity of Mrs Llewellyn's. 'She never really suffered. She was looking forward to Christmas.' We all agree, standing in the puddled car park.

I tell Charlotte that she must come and see me if she is lonely. I tell her how Mrs Llewellyn would have wanted to die at home, with her there, if she had known.

'She said a funny thing, Mrs Dove,' says Charlotte, tentatively. 'When I said goodnight to her, and told her not to worry about the washing, and to have a good sleep, like you said, she said "Goodnight, Charlotte, I think you know that I shall pray for my wings."'

Bright little sentence; single lapse. Mrs Llewellyn would not have liked it to be repeated. I say briskly, 'That shows she loved you best, Charlotte, her saying that, just to you.' I shall not tell Lesley Boakes, who is returning to make an inventory of the bungalow left to her father. I shall tell no-one. She had a good innings, Mrs Llewellyn.

Kinderspiel

Fred Urquhart

S andy's first stage appearance was at the age of twelve. It
was in 1925 in a kinderspiel in the church hall of a fishing
village on the outskirts of Edinburgh. Sandy and his three
young brothers were coerced into taking part in *Pearl the Fisher
Maiden* by their granny, their mother and their mother's
unmarried sisters, Auntie Nell and Auntie Dorothy. The three
younger Meldrum boys, Gavin, Willie and Jock, did not want
to be in it; they knew it meant the loss of at least one night's
freedom for rehearsals every week for two or three months.
Besides, they thought dressing up and singing in front of the
villagers and their friends and relations was sissy. 'There's
nothing sissy about it,' their grandmother, Mrs Gloag, told
them. 'Your Uncle Joe and your Uncle Tod and your Uncle
Willie were all in kinderspiels long ago when they were your
age. Tod was the Emperor in *Princess Chrysanthemum* and he
was in *The Princess of Poppyland* and –'

'Tod was never in *The Princess of Poppyland*, Mother,'
Auntie Nell chimed in. 'Dorothy and me were in that one, but
Tod was in *The Diamond Princess of Amsterdam*. He was the
Wicked Uncle, remember? And he was in *Princess of the South
Seas*. He was the Cannibal King. Oh, what a laugh yon one
was! Me and Dorothy were in the chorus and wore straw skirts
and had our faces blackened with burnt cork and –'

'No matter,' Mrs Gloag said. 'That has nothing to do with
thae laddies goin' into *Pearl the Fisher Maiden*. I've told Mr
Annan they'll be in it, and be in it they will.'

Sandy, always the odd man out of the Meldrum boys, was
glad to be in the kinderspiel. It would give him a chance to

48

dress up. He loved nothing better and always looked forward to Hallowe'en when Auntie Nell and Auntie Dorothy could be persuaded into rigging him out in some of their old clothes so that he could go guising and pretend he was Gloria Swanson or Pola Negri or other film actresses he saw on Saturday afternoons when he and his brothers went on the cable-tram to one of the picture houses in Edinburgh or Leith. Appearing in the kinderspiel would be like a long drawn-out Hallowe'en. And as rehearsals would be on Friday nights it meant that, afterwards, there would be fish and chips at Granny's before the long walk home in the dark, up the East Road, past the sawmills and down the Tinkers' Brae, and then they would have a long lie in bed each Saturday morning. Sandy loved a long lie as much a he loved dressing up.

Sandy's father, Alec Meldrum, was gardener at the Big House nearly half an hour's walk from the village. They used to live in Fife, where he and the other three were born, but eighteen months ago they'd come here. Sandy knew Daddy didn't like the job; he didn't get on with the mistress, Mrs Baxendale, who kept piling extra work on him. He had heard Daddy say he'd fain throw his cap over the windmill and tell Mrs Baxendale to go to hell, but he daren't. Jobs were hard to get nowadays, and with four growing laddies to feed he had to keep his bile down and his mouth shut. Any road, Daddy said, he quite liked the old Colonel, who was a gentleman, and he had a soft spot for Miss Alison.

Sandy, too, had a soft spot for Miss Alison Baxendale. She wore such lovely clothes, he could have looked at her all day. He wished he were a lassie so that when he grew up he could wear tussore suits with short skirts and a big red straw picture hat like Miss Alison, and long strings of bright coloured beads that dangled sometimes down to her knees, and lots and lots of bangles and long pearl earrings. If only he were as old as Miss Alison and dressed like her he'd go to London or Hollywood and go on the films. He wouldn't bide here with only a jaunt into Edinburgh in the car about twice a week to keep her going. He'd be like Miss Alison's brother, Mr Daniel. Mr Daniel was the oldest, of course, but he'd kicked up his heels and gone off years ago because he couldn't stand his mother's domineering ways. The Colonel had wanted Mr Daniel to bide in the army after the war, but Mr Daniel wasn't having any.

He had money of his own, left by an uncle, and he didn't need a job, so he'd gone off to North Africa and other places to enjoy himself. Sandy had seen Mr Daniel only once, but he often thought about him. Mr Daniel was big and nice-looking and had grand long legs on him. Sandy liked the way he tossed back his bonnie fair hair when he laughed, but Sandy's mother said Mr Daniel could be doing with a good haircut. Daddy said Mr Daniel was a bit of a lad, and good luck to him; but Ma always sniffed and said Mr Daniel should bide at home and not be such a thorn in his mother's side, poor old lady. Mrs Baxendale might be a hard taskmaster and a bit of a bitch but she deserved better than Mr Daniel as her only son.

The first rehearsal of *Pearl the Fisher Maiden* was in early September. Sandy arrived at the church hall about seven o'clock with his brothers and Auntie Dorothy, who, like a few other members of the choir, was going to help Arthur Annan, the young church organist, to keep the bairns in order. Dorothy shepherded the Meldrum boys into a row of cane-bottomed chairs in the middle of the hall, then went on to the platform to speak to Mr Annan, who was sitting at the piano watching them all come in.

Arthur Annan was courting Dorothy in a tentative way, rather like a hovering bird inspecting a hedge to see whether it will build a nest there or not. He had taken her twice to the pictures, the dearest seats, and they had canoodled in the hall's doorway several times after choir practice. But his suit was hanging fire. He was nervous about being brought into the ramifications of the Gloag family, with Dorothy's married brothers and sisters and their crowds of children, all stemming from the pivot of Mrs Jemima Gloag, that vigorous bigot who'd been a widow for twenty years and acted as both mother and father to her flock. Arthur Annan was not sure whether he wanted Mrs Gloag as a mother-in-law, powerful pillar of the kirk though she was.

Mr Annan's pleasant good-looking face was disfigured by thick spectacles that made him look a little owl-like, but the spectacles were really a blessing at times like this; nobody knew where he was looking. While Dorothy talked to him, he watched the children come in in twos and threes. Some small ones were accompanied by their mothers. Arthur Annan knew most of them; they came to the Sunday School, and many had been in his infant class. But there were about a dozen boys and girls who didn't attend Sunday School; they were here just for a caper. They were at this rehearsal, and maybe they'd come to the next, but soon they'd find other ploys to take up their gangrel attention.

By ten past seven about forty children had arrived. Mr Annan and his choir-ladies and the mothers decided no more potential performers were likely, so the rehearsal started. While Mr Annan was telling the children the story of Pearl, the fisher maiden who marries a prince, his helpers handed out printed copies of the kinderspiel to the older ones. They were doing this when five late-comers breenged in and sat in the row of chairs in front of the Meldrum boys. They were biggish louts of fourteen or fifteen; all had left school and were waiting to become deckhands on trawlers or greasers and shunters on the local railway line. They had no intention of appearing in the kinderspiel but were here for a lark. They shuffled about and whispered and guffawed all the time Arthur Annan played the kinderspiel's principal songs and he and the choir-ladies sang the words, urging the children to join in. While practising the choruses the louts, who came from the fishermen's cottages on the foreshore, joined in loudly, stopping every now and then to sing different, usually ribald words and laugh. After about half an hour of this, one of them broke wind with great force between choruses. 'That was a real corker,' Gavin whispered to Sandy, putting his hand over his mouth to stifle his giggles. Sandy was so embarrassed that he flushed, hoping nobody would think he was to blame. 'That boy pumped,' little Jock said in a loud voice to Auntie Dorothy. 'The teacher should give him the belt.'

The guilty lout rose grinning and put up his hand. 'Please for leave, teacher,' he called to Mr Annan. 'Please for leave.' Without waiting to hear if the organist would answer he swaggered to the door. His companions cheered and gave him rousing raspberries. At the door he lifted his leg with exaggerated slowness and farted again. Then he returned his friends' raspberries, opened the door and was gone.

Mr Annan rose from the piano. He pointed at the four remaining fisher lads and shouted: 'Out! Out, the lot of you!'

Rocking with ribald laughter, they held onto each other's shoulders as they staggered to the door. Sandy squirmed with embarrassment for Arthur Annan. Mr Annan sat down again and said: 'Now, we'll try the next chorus.'

At the end of the rehearsal Arthur Annan stopped Sandy before he followed Auntie Dorothy, Gavin, Willie and Jock through the door. He handed him a copy of the kinderspiel and said: 'I'm not going to choose who's going to play the parts until next week, Sandy, but I'd like you to take the part of the Court Jester. It's quite a big part and you've got to sing two songs. D'you think you could manage it?'

Sandy nodded. He could barely whisper: 'Yes, Mr Annan,' he was so excited. And he liked Mr Annan so much he wished he was able to say: 'Yes, Uncle Arthur.' Auntie Dorothy was a right lucky-bag to get such a nice man.

He ran to catch up with his aunt and brothers. 'I'm to be the jester,' he cried, catching Auntie Dorothy's arm and swinging against her. 'Willn't that be just great?'

'D'you mean to tell me that Arthur Annan has picked you for the part without telling me first?' Dorothy Gloag was full of umbrage. 'The sleekit so-and-so. By jings, just wait till I see him, I won't half give him a piece of my mind.'

At Granny's the usual Friday night family party was already in full swing. Two of Sandy's young uncles had been to the fish-and-chips van which came from Leith every night and parked in the village square. They'd brought back nineteen paper bags of fish suppers. Granny had put five of them in the oven. And when Dorothy screeched like a peahen: 'Mother, what d'you think of this?' Mrs Gloag silenced her with: 'Time enough for your news, Dorothy. Let me dole out thae suppers first, so long as they're hot.'

Sandy took his greasy poke of fish and chips and went behind the sofa, fully occupied by two large uncles and two small cousins, and sat on a stool that had a pile of newspapers on top. He had just put the first hot fat chip in his mouth when he heard his mother skirl: 'But our Sandy cannie sing!'

'Of course our Sandy cannie sing, Betsy,' Granny said. 'We all know that to our cost. Sandy's like his poor father, he has to go outside to get the air. He doesn't get it off our side of the family, thank God. Our side's all grand singers. It's a good job your three youngest take after us, Betsy. It would be awful if they were all like Sandy.'

'The very idea of wee Sandy bein' the jester!' Uncle Jimmy said. 'I help my kilt, it would be funny if it wasn't so serious. The jester has to sing a lot. I mind our Frank was the jester ten, maybe twelve years ago, and he used to deeve the life out of us all practisin' his songs.'

'Oh, but our Frank's a braw singer,' Granny said. 'Not like poor wee Sandy. Our Frank sang in the Usher Hall with Mr Godfrey's choir.'

'But Granny I promised Mr Annan I'd take the part,' Sandy cried.

'Well, you cannie take it,' Granny said. 'You cannie sing, and that's an end of it. There's no good goin' against the grain. You'll tell Mr Annan next week that you'll take the part of the Lord Chamberlain instead. That's a nice part for you with no singin', and you have a fine long speech to make in the third act. We just can't have you standin' up there on that platform making a fool of yourself by singin' and bringin' disgrace on the family.'

'I'll tell Arthur Annan to give the jester to somebody else when I see him on Sunday,' Dorothy said.

'You'll do no such thing,' Mrs Gloag said. 'You will not bring up the subject of a kinderspiel on the Lord's Day. Sandy will tell Mr Annan himself next Friday.'

'But he asked me,' Sandy cried. 'And I want to be the jester.'

'Don't argue with your granny, boy,' Uncle Jimmy said. 'You are not goin' to be the jester and bring disgrace on us all, so that's an end of it.'

The following Friday when Sandy told Arthur Annan, the organist said he'd already given the part of the Lord Chamberlain to Geordie Drysdale. 'With all respect to Mrs Gloag,' he said, 'I see no reason why you shouldn't be the jester. You've got a lively face, and I'm sure you're the best one for the part: you're the cleverest. C'mon, let's hear you singing.' He drew Sandy to the piano, sat down and began to play one of the jester's songs. Sandy, who'd often heard the family sing the words, started to sing nervously, but his voice strengthened as Mr Annan made no jeering comment or held his hands to his ears, which were the favourite tactics of his mother, granny, aunts and uncles. 'I don't think you sound too bad,' the organist said at the finish. 'I can't see what all the fuss is about.

You're not a Caruso or a Jack Buchanan, of course, but you'll get by. I think you'll do fine for the jester, so what about it?'

'I'd like to,' Sandy said.

'Well, you give Mrs Gloag my compliments and tell her I want you to play the part. You're the only one in the village who's suitable. And you can tell her, too, that I think you'll be a great success.'

'The man's mad,' Mrs Gloag said. 'Nobody in their sane senses would ever let you stand up in front of an audience and sing whether you've got a suitable face or no'. We're not goin' to let you bring disgrace on the family, so you can just tell Mr Annan that you won't be the jester. If he hasn't got another part for you, then you can always be one of the brigands like your wee brothers. Maybe he'll make you the brigands' chief. You won't be heard behind a newspaper singin' in the chorus, and then we can all breathe in peace.'

'But I'm too auld to be a brigand,' Sandy said. 'Everybody 'll laugh at me.'

'No' as much as they'd laugh if you were the jester. You that cannie sing a note. Now that's enough. I've a good mind to draw my hand across your jaw for defying me like this.'

'I'll do it for ye, Mother,' Uncle Tod said. 'The young pup needs a good lickin'.'

'If you lay a hand on him, Tod Gloag,' Sandy's mother said, 'I won't be answerable for what I'll do to you, big though you are. If anybody's going to lick him it'll be me or his father. So you can put that in your pipe and smoke it, bighead.'

'There's no call to go on like that, Betsy,' her mother said. 'Tod was just standin' up for the family's good name. We're not goin' to let a wee shaver like your Sandy make a laughin' stock of us.'

'Now you remember what I told you, Sandy Meldrum,' she said. 'You tell Mr Annan you're going to be a brigand. Tell him if there's any more nonsense I'll come to the hall and give him a good piece of my mind – in front of the whole lot of you. He wouldn't like that, I'll warrant.'

Sandy's mother said: 'C'mon, you kids, it's time we hit the trail.'

'Ay, Betsy, take that boy home before he causes any more mischief,' Mrs Gloag said. 'Settin' up cheek to his granny and disturbin' the whole house. If his father was half a man he'd give him a good leathering.'

Mrs Meldrum ranted about her brother Tod all the way home, but even she was silenced when her husband told her that Mr Wallace, the chauffeur, had got the sack. 'The mistress wanted him to clean the windows in the big house,' Alec Meldrum said. 'There must be over seventy of them, big and small. So Mr Wallace told the old lady it wasn't his place to do housework and if the maids wouldn't clean them she'd better hire a young fellow as an odd-jobs man. She gave him his marchin' orders, and she was all for him leavin' tonight, bag and baggage. But Mr Wallace stood up for his rights and said he'd work out his month's notice or he'd have the law on her.'

'Poor man, a lot of good that'd do him,' Betsy Meldrum said.

'And that's not all,' Alec said. 'Mr Daniel's comin' for a visit next week, and he's bringin' a horse with him. He's going hunting with the Haddington Fox Hunt. The mistress told me it'll be put in the old stable, and I'm to feed and groom it.'

'Where have you got time to groom a horse?'

'That's what I asked her, but she said did I want to follow Mr Wallace down the road, so I held my tongue.'

'It's high time Mr Daniel got married,' Betsy said. 'He needs a wife to take up his attention instead of all this nonsense about hunting foxes and going abroad. He's twenty-nine: time he settled down and behaved himself.'

Even his excitement at Mr Daniel's advent did not prevent Sandy from brooding all week-end over his granny and the kinderspiel. Although he went to church and Sunday School as usual, he did not go afterwards to Granny's with his brothers; he went home alone, taking the longer way along the beach. Slouching moodily, kicking at the pebbles, stopping occasionally to skiff flat stones into the sea, he thought about being the jester. He had already learned some of the jester's lines, and he said them over and over to himself. If Uncle Arthur – Mr Annan – said he was a good enough singer, he couldn't see why the rest didn't. It was all because of Granny forever boasting about Uncle Tod's grand voice and Uncle Frank's. Why had everybody to do what Granny told them? He didn't see why they should go to kirk and Sunday School every week just to please her. He wished he were Daddy who went to kirk only when he felt inclined. Granny called it setting a bad example, but Daddy didn't care. Granny was like old Mrs Baxendale, she wanted it all her own way.

Mr Daniel had arrived when Sandy came home from school on Tuesday. He was talking to Daddy beside a horse-box in the old stable-yard. Sandy lingered about, looking at Mr Daniel with admiring eyes, hoping he'd take notice. All that Mr Daniel did, though, was to smile and wave before he and Daddy went into the stable. Mr Daniel was so tall it seemed to Sandy he'd need to stoop to get through the doorway. There was plenty of room to spare, however. Sandy longed to follow them inside so that he could stand close to Mr Daniel and look up at him; but he didn't dare in case Daddy got angry with him for being familiar with the gentry.

After tea Sandy went to the stable to look at the horse, hoping Mr Daniel would be there. He wasn't. The horse, a heavy hunter, a bay gelding of over sixteen hands, was in the loose-box. The door into the loose-box had iron bars on its top half. Sandy admired the horse through the bars. The horse came up inquisitively to the door and pressed his nose between the bars, breathing on Sandy. Sandy put his hand on the horse's nose and stroked him. He stood stroking the velvet of the horse's muzzle for nearly an hour, murmuring endearments, but he did not dare open the loose-box door, and Mr Daniel never came.

Sandy haunted the stable for the next two nights, but there was no sign of Mr Daniel. He heard his father tell his mother that Mr Daniel had ridden the horse several times along the beach towards Cramond but had done nothing about rubbing him down afterwards. Daddy complained that he had to get up a bit earlier each morning to feed the horse and groom him. Sandy wished he was old enough to do this, but he didn't dare suggest it.

On Friday his three brothers did not come home with Sandy after school. They went to Granny's for tea. Sandy went home alone, and when his mother expressed surprise he said he had some home lessons to do and didn't want to take his school-bag to the kinderspiel rehearsal. After tea he pretended to do some homework for about twenty minutes; then he slipped his copy of *Pearl the Fisher Maiden* up the front of his jersey, and

then fastened the belt of his short trousers more tightly over
the jersey so that the copy could not fall down. His trousers
were getting too small; they'd soon have to be passed on to
Gavin, or maybe to Willie, they were so tight. He went to the
stable to look for Mr Daniel.

Although the horse whinnied a welcome there was no sign
of his young master. After caressing the horse's muzzle for a
while, Sandy looked around hesitantly, then, suddenly full of
confidence, he opened the loose-box door and went inside. He
patted the horse's neck and withers, drawing his hands lov-
ingly over the animal's chest and sides. The horse seemed
pleased to receive this attention; he nuzzled Sandy's shoulder.
The boy sensed he was looking for a titbit, and he whispered:
'I'm sorry, horse, I've nothing for you.'

The horse moved over to the manger and snuffled up the
remains of some oats. Sandy admired the swing of the big
haunches. The glossy sheen of the hide and the ripple of the
horse's muscles fascinated him. He wanted to stroke the
gleaming rump, faintly dappled by darker markings, but he
was afraid he might get kicked.

Sandy felt the need to pee, and he opened his spaver. His
water was making the straw rustle when he sensed someone
behind him. Mr Daniel came into the loose-box.

Sandy blushed guiltily. 'It's all right, boy,' Mr Daniel said,
gripping his shoulder and holding him. 'No need to run away.
You've put an idea in my head. I'd better have a run-off
too.'

Sandy, whose own flow had stopped with fright, looked
with wonder at what Mr Daniel unfurled from his tight white
riding breeches. He tried to look elsewhere, but his eyes
remained fixed. Mr Daniel still held his shoulder, so he could
not move away. Watching the stream hitting the side of the
loose-box, Mr Daniel said: 'Andrew, isn't it?'

'Sandy,' the boy whispered.

Mr Daniel smiled down at him: 'How old are you, Sandy?'

'Twelve,' he stammered. 'I must go now, Mr Daniel, or I'll
be late. I've got to go to the church hall for the kinderspiel.'

'What kinderspiel? It's German, y'know. Kinder for child,
and spiel for play. You know that, Sandy? What's this child's
play called and what're you doing in it?'

Sandy told him: 'Mr Annan wants me to be the jester, but

Granny and my mother and my uncles say I can't sing. I've to
tell Mr Annan tonight that I'll be a brigand instead.'

'Do you want to be a brigand?'

Sandy shook his head. 'I want to be the jester, but they say
I've got to go outside to get the air. I must go, Mr Daniel. I'll
have to run quite a bit to get there in time.'

'I'll take you on the horse,' Mr Daniel said. 'Would you like
that?'

Sandy nodded, his eyes wide with happiness.

'Have you ever been on a horse?'

'No,' Sandy whispered, afraid that the big young man
would change his mind.

'There's a first time for everything,' Mr Daniel said.

Mr Daniel bridled the horse and saddled him. As he bent
down to fasten the girth and then to tighten it, his backside was
only a foot from Sandy's face. The boy could not take his eyes
away from the smooth white-encased buttocks, and he had a
great desire to stroke them as he'd desired to stroke the horse's
rump. He put his hands behind him and strained against
the wall. Mr Daniel looked round and winked; then he
straightened up and said: 'Ready, boy?'

He lifted Sandy on to the horse's withers. 'Hold tight and
lean over his neck,' he said before starting to lead the horse out.
Sandy experienced a moment of terror as he looked down and
saw how far he was above the ground. He clung to the horse's
neck until they got outside. The mane grazing his cheek and
the sliding of his bare legs against the dark rippling shoulders
gave him a queer sensation.

Mr Daniel swung into the saddle, put his right arm around
Sandy and drew him against himself until the boy's legs were
lying partly on his own thick thighs. 'The tide's in, so we can't
have a gallop along the beach,' Mr Daniel said, turning the
horse's head onto the slope of the Tinkers' Brae. 'We'll take it
easy up here. There's plenty of time for you to get to the hall
before seven.'

Mr Daniel's bridle-hand was lying between Sandy's legs. As
they went up the Tinkers' Brae, he gently kneaded the boy's
crotch with his knuckles, then he slipped his thumb under the
short trousers and moved it slowly backwards and forwards.
Sandy quivered with fright and pleasure at the peculiar sensation in his groin. A pulse began to throb in his bottom; it was

like one of the small pistons he'd seen moving in the engine of the ferry-boat *The William Muir* and he hoped it would never stop. He put his hands on Mr Daniel's knees and he turned his head and pressed his cheek against the young man's chest. Daniel laughed and rubbed his chin on top of the boy's head.

'You're not ready yet, Sandy,' he said.

Outside the church hall Daniel dismounted and lifted Sandy from the horse. 'You all right, boy?' he asked. 'You haven't got your legs grazed against his hide? The next time you come riding with me you'd better wear longer trousers.'

He smiled at the adoration in the boy's eyes. He pinched Sandy's cheek and said: 'You'll soon be ready, boy.'

He swung back into the saddle. Gathering up the reins he said: 'Now don't forget what I told you, Sandy. You be the jester and damn the consequences.'

He grinned, waved and cantered off towards the Granton road. Sandy stood for a few minutes looking after the white curves above the darker ones as they grew smaller and smaller, then he went up the hall's steps. His mind was made up. He was going to be what Daniel wanted him to be.

The Girl in the Mad Hat

Dorothy Goulden

Diana stood at the barrier and watched the train disappearing from view. Disconsolately she turned away. She had missed it by seconds and she hated being late for the office. Then she thought of the letter in her bag. It was from her son, Stephen. She had longed to open it before she left the house, but there was not time. Now she could read it over and over again in that long wait before the next train.

Hugging the thought to herself, she went over to the form opposite the barrier. A young girl, already sitting there, made room for her. Diana had a confused impression of gleaming spectacles and a moon-shaped, anxious face.

'I'm sorry,' said the girl. 'I do seem to take up a lot of room.'

A bulging plastic bag and a cartwheel hat lay between them on the seat. 'I don't want to crush your hat,' said Diana. She opened her bag and took out the letter.

'Dear Mother,' she read. 'I'm sorry to be so long in writing. As you see from the address, I have moved. I am on the fifth floor of this grotty house, but never mind . . .'

'I'll move this out of your way.' The girl picked up the plastic bag and deposited it on the floor.

'Don't worry,' murmured Diana.

'The landlord has promised to mend the roof. You must come for the weekend when I'm straight. There's a smashing view from here – you would love it.'

The girl's voice was soft and insistent. 'I thought I'd lost my ticket.'

Diana turned the page. 'I've heard nothing about that job I told you about. How are things with *you*?'

62

'But I found it in the bottom of my handbag. Do *you* ever do things like that?'

Diana looked up. 'Will you excuse me,' she said. 'I'm trying to read.'

The girl had great dark eyes behind the spectacles. She beamed happily at Diana and chatted on. 'I'm always losing things. When I go anywhere, I keep tight hold of my bag. If I don't, I leave it on the train or the bus.'

Diana looked at her watch. There were ten more minutes before the train. 'That's very sensible of you,' she said, and deliberately turned her shoulder.

'Have you thought any more about getting a car? I don't know how you stand that train journey.'

It was useless to read. The girl was shuffling her feet on the concrete floor. Diana stared down, hypnotized. They were large feet, encased in red sandals.

'Are you admiring my sandals?' The girl stuck her legs out stiffly in front of her – strong, sturdy legs, uncompromisingly plump.

'They're very pretty sandals,' said Diana gravely.

'My mum bought them for me last week. She said I needed a pair to go away with.'

She swung her feet up and down, admiring the sandals. Diana watched her. She had dark hair, cut short just below the ears and curving down from a centre parting. Her round face had a strange, two-dimensional effect; Diana suddenly remembered a rag doll she had been given as a child.

Beyond the barrier a train had just drawn in. Doors were opening, people alighting on the platform. Diana got up thankfully. 'I do believe this is my train,' she said, gathering up her bag and the precious letter.

'Are you going to Slindon Junction?' said the girl. 'Could I travel with you? Please?'

She stood up. Her cotton skirt stood out stiffly, away from her body. In one hand she held the cartwheel hat; a garish flower drooped raggedly over the brim. The plastic bag sagged from her other hand, almost touching the floor. She was a large girl and towered over Diana like a grotesque doll.

The people from the incoming train crowded through the barrier. Diana watched them disperse along the concourse; young girls, shining spruce in their chainstore clothes; women

with powdered faces, avidly talking to each other; young men
with non-committal eyes. She wanted to cry out for help, but
they were work-a-day crowds. The unpredictable only happened at weekends at the touch of a button.

'Your bag is trailing on the floor,' she said sharply. The
girl's eyes filled with tears. Diana looked away.

She waited until the last person cleared the barrier. The
ticket collector nodded and waved her on as she produced her
season ticket. Her heels clicked along the platform. Behind
her, the girl struggled and gasped, dropping her bag, showing
the wrong ticket, rag doll face red with exertion.

'I ought to help her,' thought Diana. 'But I can't. It would
give her a claim on me.'

The girl caught her up. 'I can't keep up with you. Are you
sure you don't mind me travelling with you?'

Diana ignored this. 'Come on, we'll get in here. It's a
non-smoker.'

It was an old-fashioned compartment with a corridor at one
end and two long seats facing each other. Diana settled herself
in a corner seat. The girl sat down opposite, her skirt bunched
round her solid figure. The plastic bag bulged and splayed out
on the seat beside her.

'Why don't you put your things on the rack?' said Diana.
Then reluctantly, 'Here, let me help you.'

'Oh no, I mustn't do that.' The girl clutched the brim of her
hat. 'I might leave them on the train. I told you. I do that
sometimes. My mum gets ever so cross.'

Diana stared out of the window. It was almost time to go.
There was a flurry of passengers, a slamming of doors and the
guard blew his whistle. Too late, Diana realized that she and
the girl were alone in the compartment. This ridiculous girl
with her wet eyes and vapid face. She would tell Stephen about
it. 'Oh, go on,' he would say. 'You're a soft touch.'

The train slid smoothly out of the station, past the sidings
with their conglomeration of trucks and along the track that
curved round to the viaduct.

'Where are you going?'

'I'm not telling you,' thought Diana. Aloud she said, 'I
change trains at Slindon Junction.'

'I'm going to stay with my friend. I have to catch a bus when
I leave the train.'

Diana gazed out at the view from the viaduct. Down below, row upon row of houses stretched away to the skyline. An arterial road cut through the patchwork of densely packed terraces. It was a familiar scene to Diana, but this morning every outline stood out sharply as if she had extra vision. She saw a group of people standing at a zebra crossing. The traffic waited and they crossed. Further along, the same traffic stopped at a set of traffic lights. Seen from the viaduct it was like a silent movie with the rhythm of the train making an accompaniment.

'My friend – you know, the friend I'm staying with – belongs to a funny religious sect. They all wear hats.'

Diana turned her head. 'I beg your pardon.'

'They all have to wear hats.' The girl's eyes shone with pleasure at Diana's incredulity.

'What, all of them?'

'No, not the men, just the women. I don't know what they are. Just a funny religious lot. They're strict about wearing hats. That's why I bought one.'

She poked at the artificial flower on the brim, pulling it to shreds.

'It's a very large brim,' said Diana. 'Do they wear hats all the time?'

The girl shook her head. 'No, only when they go out. But that's bad enough. It's a mad house, what with their hats and everything. The women aren't allowed to wear trousers, only dresses. My friend wants to wear jeans and go to discos. It's a shame. *My* mum doesn't mind what I wear.'

They had left the built-up area. The houses backing on to the railway line had gardens and proud new extensions. Diana saw a woman bending over a flower bed, watched by two small children.

The girl began to rummage through her plastic bag. It fell sideways on the seat, spilling out a pink brassière and a toilet bag. The cartwheel hat slid off her knee; Diana picked it up. The ribbon round the brim was black with grime.

'How long are you staying with your friend?' she said.

'I'm staying for two days.' The words came out in a rush. 'After that my boyfriend is coming to pick me up. He came to see me last night but I was out and when I got back he'd left, so

my mum said I would be leaving my friends the day after
tomorrow and that's why he's picking me up then.'

She stopped, breathless. Her eyes never left Diana's face.

'He's ever so nice. We've known each other since I was
fourteen. We might get married. My parents won't mind – I
don't think they will.'

Diana felt a great drowsiness. There were people talking in
the next compartment but they sounded a long way off.

'You're very lucky,' she said mechanically, not caring.

The train rushed through Blatchington Halt. Through the
window she saw a steep embankment, covered with lush
foliage. 'Look at the flowering valerian. The roots of the plant
make people sleepy and cats hysterical. Stephen is great on
herbs, he told me.'

She thought she had said the words aloud, but the girl was
still talking. 'My mum's ever so nice. She's got a shaggy perm
and she wears pencil skirts. She dresses really young. Not like
my friend's mum.'

The train rushed through a tunnel and for fifteen seconds
Diana's ears were filled with a roaring sound. The girl watched
her, eyes bright in the electric light. Then it was daylight and
her voice came out of the roaring. 'My friend's mum is nice,
ever so homely. She's got her hair in a sort of roll – my mum
says she ought to do herself up a bit more – but she's nice, my
friend's mum. She lets me put all my stuff in the bathroom
when I stay with them. It's not her fault about the religious
stuff and all that.'

'I never said it was,' said Diana.

'It's my friend's dad, he's very strict.'

'I'm getting out soon,' said Diana.

There was a burst of laughter from the next compartment.

'The people next door are laughing at us,' said the girl.

'No, they're not,' said Diana, sitting up straight and
reaching for her bag. 'Now, look, you're trailing your hat
ribbon on the floor.'

'They're laughing at us. They're laughing at you as well as
me.' The girl made no attempt to wipe away the tears rolling
down her cheeks.

There was a great hurrying and commotion as the train
drew in at Slindon Junction. Diana got up to open the carriage
door, then hesitated.

'Nobody is laughing at us,' she said. 'I must leave you now. I'm late.'

'Don't go. Please – please –' The girl gripped her arm and pulled her back from the door. People stood about on the platform; a voice over the tannoy announced the departure of the train; no-one got into the compartment. Diana struggled to free herself, but she was in a grip of steel. 'Let go, you great – stupid lump – let go of my arm –'

In one movement the girl turned her round and pushed her down the seat. The force behind the push made Diana gasp. 'You stupid girl,' she said weakly. 'I'll be carried on to – the next station. Oh, you stupid girl.'

The train slid out of the junction and along the glittering tracks that lay beyond. The girl put her hands on Diana's shoulders, pressing her down on the seat.

'You called me stupid. And I thought you were my friend. I thought you were ever so nice. Even when you wanted to read your silly letter.'

Diana stared up at the wet dark eyes behind the spectacles. She started to cry.

Bright Star

Margaret Browne

Even now when the fields in France are ploughed they still find unexploded shells. Jason, my brother, was killed in the first half of the Somme.

'Like mayflies,' murmured my mother, her gentle face puffed with tears.

Our farmhouse seemed bigger than ever and more frightening after Jason died for England and a shilling a day. To me, a child at school, death was a far-off country but now a sudden creak on the stair would make me remember him. Shapes seemed to move at night, a bullying wind would make the starlings shift and squeal under the eaves, short-eared owls would skitter on the roof. Each night full of whispers. Ghosts are subtle, rob the living of peace of mind. They have skeletons of steel.

The day I met Wrangler, the gypsy, I was returning from school. I dawdled to watch the cormorants on the river. They had stood holding up grey-black wings to a lean February sun which had streaked through the gathering clouds. In absorbed silence I watched, my boots soaking up half the river. Wrangler must have come to the lip of the wood, slim, quiet as an adder. I would have moved on but the creature in his arms stopped me in his tracks. Excitement, curiosity, jerked me forward to meet him.

'She's a beauty!' I said.

It was a ferret. A wild surge of joy shot through my body as my hand touched the soft sandy fur. Fine head, tiny feet black as dancing pumps.

'How much will you give me for her then?'

I looked up into Wrangler's shrewd brown eyes. Silhouetted against the light he was much taller than me but not as old as Jason had been. I felt in my pocket, finding a two shilling piece, a few coppers of little value and the round silver watch which had been given me by Jason as a keepsake. It was plain, but silver, and an excellent time-keeper. Wrangler took the watch from me, holding it carefully in his palm, the silver chain forming an elegant loop. He was delicately silent. The watch gleamed brightly in the last of the sun. The more I looked the more I didn't want him to take it yet I knew he would get a good price for such a ferret anywhere.

Wrangler smiled. A touch of Lucifer.

There was still time to refuse.

'Is it yours to barter?'

'Yes.'

'All right,' he said suddenly, dismissive as though anxious to be on his way. 'You take it. What are you going to call her?'

'Dunno,' I answered.

The warm, wriggling body was in my hands, fur soft, smooth as chiffon. The ferret was nuzzling my fingers, eyes dark, intelligent.

Wrangler left silently and vanished as swiftly as he had appeared. Now the sky was darkening, the cormorants gone. It was February, the hedging time, the mole-catching month, wayside full of Dog's Mercury, one of winter's flowers. Candlemas already gone. The woods seemed to take on a tenebrous life of their own at dusk. Feet soaked, satchel thumping my back, I reached the last stretch of road, kept only in fair repair, which led to our farm. The rooks were going to roost. High above the elms I saw the steadfast first star.

'Bright Star,' I whispered to the ferret, 'I'll call you "Bright Star".'

Turning in at our gate I counted nine pigeons on the roof, warm Ruabon tiles gleaming warm in lengthening shadows. Lights already beaming through wide kitchen windows. As I lifted the latch I noticed the japonica against the south wall was in bloom. In love with the ferret, smiling at my own daring, I felt the skins of childhood falling away. Wrangler the gypsy had a bargain but I had Bright Star.

The ferret was the most beautiful thing I ever owned.

That afternoon was imprinted on my mind forever.

★

February 11, 1980.

I'm all behind with the dusting. I stopped to speak to Sister Billington. 'Sister,' I said. 'About Mr Harvey – he doesn't seem well.'

'If he was well he wouldn't be here,' she said ever so tart. 'I know he's your favourite, Ginny, but a Nursing Home looks after people who are ill. If he was well he wouldn't be here. Don't forget he's eighty-six.'

'Eighty-five,' I answered.

'Have it your own way, then.'

'He was telling me about his brother Jason. Lost in the war. An awful lot died in that war.'

'Memories are by their nature fragmented,' she said, 'and I'd be obliged if you'd dust the top of the wardrobes more often. There's clouds of dust on some, Ginny. This spring sunshine shows it up. I must do the medication now. Doctor Stringer will be here in half an hour. Run along now, Ginny – there's a good girl.

A field of geese is always a delight. Stately, comical, white as swans. In those days goose fat was used for healing ointment, goose down fetched three shillings a pound.

Time moved on slowly.

Rumour like bindweed went around the villages. They were taking all the horses from the farms for the war.

'There'll be no statues put up for horses,' remarked my grandfather pulling hard on his pipe. 'They'll not take our horses while I'm here.'

That morning he took me to school in the trap, making his way through the fresh and innocent landscape which knew little of bomb and shell except for the prisoners-of-war who were now employed on drainage work. The almond smell of meadowsweet was on the air.

'I'm going to the cattle market,' said Grandfather as I jumped down by the school gate, but I knew it was not the truth. He rummaged in his pockets for his tobacco pouch, which was not there, then went on his way. I watched the trap disappear. I knew Grandfather was going to do something about the horses. Joseph Arch had always been his hero. The story of how Arch had stood amongst the bean poles and lanterns addressing a crowd of farm labourers was Grandfather's best story. The men put forward demands for an increase in their wages to two shillings and eightpence a day and a reduction in their hours of work. It had resulted in a strike.

There was no moon that night.

The geese woke me giving warning. I jumped out of bed pulling on my dressing-gown, hearing the beating of my own heart and hooves clattering on the cobbled yard below. The horses were being led out from the stable. I glimpsed Wrangler outlined in a winding saffron light, caught the smell of leather, the soft muskiness of horse flesh in the warm night. Wrangler was taking the horses to safety.

In the morning Grandfather sighed. He was thinking of the war.

'I'm too old and you're too young,' he said as he mended an old axe handle but he was writhing on the rack of guilt just the same. I went out and across the yard passing the empty stables.

'Say nothing,' my mother had whispered. 'They will be safe.'

No-one came for the horses. Our farm was off the beaten track, miles away from the nearest village, buried too deep in the valley. It made Grandfather jittery. His rheumy grey-blue eyes would scour the lanes for strangers and he drank more brandy. There had been no better hedger than Grandfather for some distance and his work was in much demand. Out of straggling thorns and hazel he had made stock-proof hedges but now he was no longer eager to leave our farm.

We pulled through as best we could. Factories were left without skilled men – they had worked fifty to sixty hours for as little as five shillings. Now some had the Mons Star – others a shroud. Women took their place in the factories and enjoyed the new freedom it brought.

Time passing light as a dandelion clock blown on the wind. Honey-coloured, heavy summer days. Then leaves lying, lush copper, on the white roads. I ran through the cobwebbed fields at dawn with Bright Star. Joy and freedom.

Without warning, Grandfather died.

In the war 20,000 men were being killed in one day.

Jet beads, bombazine, black crepe on hats, fine veils. The lane tracks gleaming like aspic where the funeral carriages had passed through the mud.

Carvers, wealthy but distant relatives from the market

town, came for the funeral. They owned a newspaper shop by the cattle market, a crimson and green parrot of gigantic size presided over the busy counter and paintings which they had collected. Mr Carver, whiskery and thin, smelling of hair oil and disinfectant, had once been a butler to a Lord. He moved silently and rarely spoke. His wife, Amelia, who had been a maid, stepped carefully over the farm mud, drawing her skirts about her.

Grandfather was buried at St Helen's church, best elm coffin. His room still smelling of snuff, leather, polished canisters full of white shirt buttons, medals in fine purple boxes, guns silent in strong leather cases, black ebony writing case from India – paraphernalia of nearly eighty years. Grandfather, after all his time in Africa, falling off Wyatt Bridge on his way home from the 'Stick & Weasel', found dead by the village blacksmith wearing his red carnation like a daub of blood, stiff as a brush in sheaths of river iris.

An unexpected, ignominious end for one who had rattled and roared through life unbridled as a March wind.

Grandfather's tools were put away. Hand bill, rake and crook, bagging hook. Knife which had the smell of clean, oiled metal. Wrapped carefully in newspaper, then sacking. Put away safely in the barn rafters. The newspaper rustled, whispered. It is hard to become loosened and unbound from the past, few of us ever escape.

Time passing quicker – there was so much work to get through. My mother's relatives helping on the farm. Peace. Men who served in the war were now unemployed in the towns, getting 29/– from the Labour Exchange.

Other summers. Hedges full of bright blackberries. Fool's Parsley. Two skylarks to every field, corn cockle, poppies. Night. Listening to the hall clock counting time. Order. Rhythm. Moments, globule thick. Lined with experience, full of exaggerations – thus is youth. Flutter of white outside. White as hoar frost. Barn owl. Eyes yellow saucers. Scream lost in the depth of pillow, trapped in blue eiderdown forever. An object rattling, falling.

February 12, 1980.
I'm all behind with the cleaning this morning. Not in the right mood. Inanimate objects have a will of their own. Mr

Harvey has dropped his glasses again and his magnifying glass – you would have thought the clatter would have woken him up. I'll place them on here by the photograph of his wife. He was married twice. I think his first wife died. They had three children in all. He's told me a lot about himself.

I've found a new job. I've been waiting to tell Sister Billington but now she's gone to the bank before they close. I don't know how I'm going to tell Mr Harvey. I've got quite fond of him. But I only get a pound an hour in this place and I really don't like it. There's staff changes all the time. There's that thrush singing in the tree out there. Mr Harvey often sits by the window so he can watch the birds . . . such a sweet strong song has the thrush . . .

I hated winter. I was up in the morning while the moon still shone, the countryside stretched out blue and white with hoar frost. I dreamt of Jason quite often. The dreams were like fuzzy photographs – unclear but there just the same. I found an old penknife in the stables which belonged to him – perhaps that's what started it off. There's a grave somewhere in France which is his. It was a futile war.

The winter of my twenty-third year was a bad one. The lake which lay between us and the village froze hard. People came from miles around – not just the villages but the towns as well. They skated until dusk, the trees dark, tendrilled against the sky, the onyx dusk lingering. That was when I first met Letty.

Three years later we were married at St Helens – rose yard glorious in June. Letty arriving at the farm, four tea chests of china, pug dog frightening the life out of the farm cats. Bone china replacing farm cups. Lavender instead of snuff in Grandfather's old room. The heavy atmosphere was ripped. Letty passed easily amongst the ghosts, graceful, fresh as a flower.

Gypsies came round as they had done before. Snowdrops, willow pegs, wooden flowers. Letty, not as charitable as my mother, bought them at the door, then threw them away in case of germs. Twice, during the second summer of my marriage – perhaps the third – I saw Wrangler in the distance, a lurcher at his heels, yet I found no snares in meadow or copse. I was so busy I had no thought to look elsewhere. Time had thrust itself between me and Wrangler. And now Jason too.

The old wooden stairs, the spine of the farm, was rebuilt. It creaked no longer on winter nights.

Nothing is permanent but it seemed my happiness with Letty would never dull. A tranquillity, not known before, never imagined, pervaded my life. The seasons were good, labour easy to find. The thatcher coming each August, corn a gigantic cloth of gold across the earth. Orchards bee-humming, my daughter Tamsin born, crisp black hair a mass of curls.

Bright Star had disappeared one morning down by the stream – all those years ago. Searching, calling, fretting – all had been of no avail. No analgesic for the pain. Intense in youth, searing. In maturity, drawn out, longer lasting. The facets of sorrow.

I lost Letty – gone with Wrangler, so some said. But then, gossip had always run like bindweed through the villages. I travelled miles, searched Horse Fairs, summer fêtes, waited by the casement at dusk idly watching the swallows return, curving, dipping against spring's pink hued sky. Wrangler had a way with animals and people.

By that April, the land was a green quilt. I still owned my own land, the farm which by right should have belonged to Jason.

Anna came from the town to look after Tamsin. Verbena in place of lavender. Years later I married Anna. Two sons, few excitements, few tears.

Then I saw the blouse on the secondhand stall in the market town. Magnolia in colour, meticulously fluted, two tiny buttons missing from the cuff. Letty had taken such a blouse with her.

'How much is this?'

The woman, dark, hairpin thin, darted towards me, hovering on the other side of the stall. People pushing past.

'Two shillings in that box – all two shillings.'

Long fine gloves which had seen better days. Fur tippets. Bright beady eyes. Reeking of camphor.

'How much the whole box?'

'A pound.'

I handed the money over. A crisp pound note. The day I had met Wrangler I had silver in my pocket but I never thought to offer him that first. Grandfather had not been obliged to cross

Wyatt Bridge. He had cleaned nearby ditches as a boy as I had. Knew the land like the back of his hand. Do we decide these things for ourselves or are we drawn on mercilessly by fate? Taking the box, feeling a fool in the crowded jostling market, I elbowed my way out. Somewhere, down by the cathedral, a thrush was singing. I thought of Letty, fair as a lily, of Wyatt Bridge. It had rusty girders, had not been safe but then the water had not been deep.

I took the box home. Beads of no value but a pair of grey gloves. Letty had worn grey gloves the evening we had met at the frozen lake.

The afternoon bled away.

I could find neither words nor tears. I thrust the past from me.

Children growing up – laughter in the orchards. Excitement strumming like wires.

Time going jack-knife fast. Children nearly adults. Two wars. Cenotaph, technology, motorways, towns swallowing up land. Face of society changing. Ugliness of the new. Carp, wych elms gone. Small things, glow-worms, watercress in the stream, vanished forever.

Our little market town was a complete world in itself. It was fast becoming a city. Both the Carvers were now dead, the parrot long gone.

One September I met Jamie in one of the busy streets. Jamie had gone to school with Jason, gone to the war and come home again. In the Second World War he had been a railway-man doing double-home jobs, driving through places like Coventry and Liverpool where the bombing had been very bad. Land-mines had blown up whole streets of houses. As he approached me, still wearing his overalls, I saw they were thick with grime and that he looked lined and old. How far we had travelled from the village school. He was full of the lore of railways, which he loved, shed cats who lived at the great railway works, his slow voice patient and kind. No mention was made of Letty, though he had been at the wedding. The past was like a buried landscape, we know it is there, but the contours are no longer sharp. For that brief time I walked the imperious borderline between the self of today and that other younger self of childhood. I'd had richer choices than Jamie.

It was Michaelmas Day. When I returned home a great flock of flying-ants had tumbled down the chimney. The haws were bright in the hedges, oak tree seedlings were everywhere. Soon the lanes would be swarming with children who still come searching for 'konkers'. Sward and leaf. Life and joy of it renewed each year . . .

February 13, 1980.
Mr Harvey was telling me this morning about the devastation by Luftwaffe at Plymouth. They dropped more than 20,000 incendiary bombs as well as high explosives. He said there were women signallers and women porters at railway goods yards. They had women working presses in sound locator factories. He said about 400 German planes flew up the Thames Estuary towards London – a lot of bombs dropped on the docks. He remembers it vividly but I can't understand why he suddenly started talking about it. It's the tablets – that's what I think – I'm against all those tablets. I told Sister Billington I was giving in my notice. She was not pleased. 'You should have given me more time' she snaps. 'You'd gone to the bank yesterday'. I said 'And the day before I didn't know I'd got the job myself.'
    'When do you want to go, Ginny?' she asked.
    'The end of the month,' I said.
    'Would you not consider staying,' she asked, 'just a little longer? We're so short staffed, short-handed. Some of the patients will really miss you . . .' The telephone started ringing. Sister Billington answered it. Someone was ringing at the front entrance bell. I had to go and open it. It's not my job to be opening the front door. Then they wonder why there's dust on top of the wardrobe. It was Mr Harvey's daughter, Tamsin. I don't know how she does it with the farm to look after – she seems to be coming almost every day now. Both his sons went abroad – Canada or some such place. No. One went to San Francisco. I recall him telling me that . . . I must get on. There's the stairs to do . . .

Time has stopped. The doldrums. Grey limbo – a mist at sea. Tepid water in glass by bed. We used to have a scarecrow to scare the rooks and pigeons. I was it when I was about ten. The arms were unable to remain stiff – they dithered between heaven and earth. The head, oval shaped, lolled. The yellow shirt gaped where the ribs should have been, straw stuck out. Imperfect. But it had the air of reality. It took in the birds. What is reality? In the hard white light of day, in the whiteness of the sheets, reality fades. Time gone, times recalled, time playing tricks, time intangible.

The yellow shirt, buttonless, collarless, belonged to Grandfather. I thought, I knew, the magnolia blouse belonged to Letty – Letty who was fair as a lily. The years of peace belonged to Anna. Sometimes I think I can still hear her voice at dusk when the striped tawny light from outside comes through the trees.

February – woods thick with Dog's Mercury.

February – the mole-catching month.

February – the time to fix the hedges.

Cormorants holding up their wings to dry in the sun. Wrangler, unfathomable, old as time, holding Jason's silver watch. Elegant loop hanging down. Time ticking away fast. A touch of Lucifer in Wrangler's smile. Bright Star. The most beautiful thing I ever owned.

Slim fingers on the silver watch face stopping.

Time ended.

February 14, 1980.

Congestive cardiac failure – thrombosis. That's what Sister Billington told me. Never seen her so upset. Not as hard as she makes out. You have to be hard in this job. I have to pack his things. I knew he was very ill. Rambling on and off when he was talking. Mentioned the stars quite often. February is a hard month on the old. Candlemas he called it. But I hoped he would see another summer. I keep on crying. Just can't get over it. His daughter asked me to go to the funeral. I think I may. Sons abroad, widower of some years standing. Not many to go to the funeral – all his real friends gone before. He was eighty-seven, so they say now.

His daughter always brought him flowers from the country lanes – not so easy to come by these days. Most of the early flowers are yellow. Gold. Promise of the spring to come. Bit of a mystery that daughter. Hair still dark as a raven though she must be getting on herself. Not a bit like Mr Harvey in appearance. Unfathomable. That's the word – unfathomable. Dark as a gypsy.

Mab's Hill

Kelvin I. Jones

There was an old woman
Lived under a hill
And if she's not gone
She's living there still.

Through a soot-stained window, the Reverend Whitaker stared out at the brown fields and narrow lanes of Herefordshire. Two hills in particular caught his interest. Their clean lines curved up and down, snake-like against the grey sky. Elsewhere the land lay flat. In the distance he could make out a hamlet, clustered about the valley floor. But it was the humped hills which filled the foreground.

The steam train careered into a short tunnel. For a moment he was plunged in darkness. When daylight resumed, he blinked uncertainly, aware that the hills of Wodenbury had shifted position. He made his way back to the compartment where pipe smoke lay in wreaths about the stale air. His fob-watch told him it was 2.15 pm precisely, three minutes from his destination.

A shaft of sunlight splashed against the compartment window, dazzling him. In less than a minute the clouds had dispersed, leaving a patch of blue. The hills reared up at him again, threatening to engulf the surrounding landscape. He extinguished his pipe and, placing a hand over his eyes, stared in amazement at the furrowed hills. Across their tops he could pick out the ancient trackway Wilson had described to him. Straight as a dye, it ran, a dark ribbon linking the valleys that lay either side of the Morrigans.

He rose and pulled his suitcase from the rack above his head. Its weight wrenched his shoulder. Inside, amongst several dark grey suits, was a small library of antiquarian books, and some others by his own hand. For the Reverend Claude Whitaker pursued two vocations – three if his passion for ancient history is to be admitted.

The station was small and unimpressive. A porter helped him to the barrier where he paused for some minutes, staring at the bare hedgerows and the ominous black rainclouds, threatening from out of a brooding January sky. He relit his pipe. Ahead, blocking out the skyline, the Morrigan hills swept upwards. Their perfection of form fascinated him.

A clatter of horses' hooves jerked him back into the present. A fly, led by a brown nag, rattled its way from behind a bend. A straw hat concealed the driver's face.

Whitaker heard the train pull out behind him. An explosion of steam drifted up from the small bridge as the fly crossed. The horse broke into a canter. Whitaker noticed a swaddled form in the back. Clearly this was Mrs Annis. Somehow he had imagined his prospective housekeeper as a small, slight woman. Mrs Annis was portly. A straw hat covered her round face and comely arms.

The driver reined the horse and helped Mrs Annis down. A sudden gust snatched at her hat and whipped it into the air. Valiantly, Whitaker caught it on its downward descent, then turned to face his housekeeper.

Close up, Mrs Annis confirmed his first impression of her. She had the fat red cheeks of a country person. Whitaker shook one of her podgy hands and smiled as the driver loaded his heavy suitcase into the fly. Mrs Annis introduced herself with a slow drawl, touching him lightly on the forearm occasionally to emphasize a point. She was sure he would find the vicarage warm and comfortable. She had laid fresh fires in all the rooms. Her manner was effusive.

The fly rattled over the bridge. The driver whistled to himself as Mrs Annis continued to talk excitedly. Ahead, Whitaker saw the tall steeple of St Bridget's, circled by a string of thatched cottages. Either side, the slopes of the Morrigan hills pressed their weight into the valley. Whitaker admired it all: the rise and fall of his housekeeper's ample chest, the clink of the iron wheels on the unmade road, the exciting sweep of the hills, broken only by the proud pinnacle of the Mother Church.

The Reverend Whitaker quickly grew accustomed to his housekeeper's solid plain cooking. Breakfast, served punctually at seven, took place in the low-beamed back parlour of the vicarage (the dining-room was reserved for the bishop and other august persons).

If his congregation lacked inspiration, the same could not be said of Whitaker's surroundings. The large four-poster bed gave him ample room, whilst the view from the bedroom window was breathtaking. More than once he stood here as the evening light waned, watching the brown hills darken magnificently against the horizon. It was a sight worthy to behold.

Sundays were his busiest days. He liked to begin early, adding the final flourishes to his sermon at a writing desk placed directly beneath the window so that he could ponder the marvels of The Creator. But there were days when he allowed himself time to explore the countryside and wander along deserted trackways. When the bishop's letter came, informing him of the new incumbency, it had seemed to him like a miracle. Alone, on quiet evenings, with only the hedgerow birds as his companions, the dream was fulfilled.

One sunlit morning in late February, he abandoned his customary paths to wander into the bell tower. Staring up at the bellropes, he recalled his first glimpse of Wodenbury. Often the image had returned to him. The bulging hills, cleft by the finger of God, epitomized some hidden strength or divine purpose he was unable to define.

He found the key. The door, fragile through age and disuse, yielded reluctantly. A series of spiral stairs wound upwards. He stood inside the door, overwhelmed by the musty smell of wood, his eyes adjusting to the darkness. He would take care for many of the steps seemed rotten or loose.

A dusty rope guided him. Another door brought him out seventy feet above the churchyard. He looked down, fearfully. Dwarf houses and ribbon fields stretched out beneath. His senses reeling, he grabbed at the lead pipe beside him for support. The view was magnificent, nevertheless. He could see the great sweep of the Morrigan Hills, built like defences about the ancient valley.

The fresh air brought a bloom to his cheeks. He lingered, drinking in the tapestry of colours, imagining that at any moment clouds might descend and crush him like an insect.

Whilst he stood, a pattern of light began to emerge. At first he put it down to imagination, but in a second he realized that he was not mistaken.

Through the cropped fields a network of lines had risen. A shape lay there, concealed beneath the topsoil. Only from this vantage point, high above the village, was this perception possible. Excitement mounted in him. He took out a pocket book and began to draw. A round face with beaked nose took shape. Behind it lay something rather like a horse. His hand trembled, barely able to manoeuvre the pencil. The discovery was his. Lost for centuries beneath the hillside, staring up at the church, lay the hill figure of Wodenbury.

In clean white vestments he stood at the graveside, staring down at the soil. The mourners had departed. Now a grey pall hung about the cemetery. It had been a sad occasion. The woman, a victim of consumption, had died young. The husband had shown him a photograph. The lean face laboured under the weight of lustreless eyes. It made him recall another funeral when he had stood at his mother's graveside, the rain lashing at his face. That cold November day often returned to him, for when the bond was severed, and his mother slid into the shadows, her determined presence vanished forever.

The click of the lych-gate broke his reverie. He glanced up, then stared with amazement. A dapper figure in a striped suit raised his hat.

'Charles!'

'Surprised to see me, Claude?'

Several weeks ago he had written to Charles Wilson but received no reply. Years had elapsed since their parting at Oxford, where Charles had shone as a brilliant student of archaeology. He explained to his old friend as they made their way to the church porch.

'Your letter was most exciting. Of course I knew of the legend of the Morrigan Hills, but no work has ever been produced to verify the existence of a hill figure. I thought I would come down and see for myself.'

Whitaker confessed ignorance of the legend. There were a number of tales about the 'giant' of the Morrigan hills, Charles Wilson revealed. He had thought them groundless.

The church was chill. As they strolled down the central nave, their footsteps ringing against the flagstones, his companion cast an experienced eye over the building. High up, beneath grotesque corbels, a horn of plenty hung. Whitaker con-

fessed to Wilson that he had never noticed it. They passed into
the Lady Chapel where a realistic oil painting depicted the suffer-
ing Virgin Mary. Placed about the altar and attached to the
frame of the painting were a number of curious shapes, plaited
from straw. Wilson picked one up and examined it, a figure
with primitive straight arms and a long broom-like dress.

'What are they?'

'Corn dollies.'

Whitaker, curious about their sighting in this part of the
church, was enlightened by his companion. Their function
was to promote fertility. In his native Oxfordshire they were
common enough.

'This one is very like a woman. How round and squat she
appears.'

Whitaker remarked on the crudity of its appearance.

They went out into the daylight. Wilson enthused about
the figure on the hill. Naturally Whitaker had read of the
unearthing of the great Celtic horse goddess in Berkshire.
Wilson's discovery had even reached the pages of the national
newspapers.

'As far as I am aware, there are no Bronze Age settlements in
the vicinity of the Morrigan Hills. This could be considerably
older.'

Their discussion continued far into the evening. Whitaker
valued his friend's visit. Of late he had grown rather introspec-
tive. He noticed a growing tendency in himself to spend
mornings in the company of Mrs Annis. This gnawed at his
conscience. Mrs Annis was a widow. Whitaker had a reputation to uphold. On warm days he would open his bedroom
window wide enough to let his foolish feelings disperse. Clean
linen and punctuality kept him close to the Lord.

The day faded. Charles Wilson was more than happy to
accept Whitaker's invitation to stay. Mrs Annis bustled about
in the visitor's bedroom, rolling back the sheets with her
ruddy hands.

As darkness engulfed the vicarage, Whitaker lay his head
against the clean starched pillow. In his mind was the image of
the Virgin Mary, her pale face stained with tears. She knelt at
the foot of the cross where the blood of Christ flowed like a
scarlet stream. His hand reached out to touch the hem of her
dress. Between his fingers he felt the texture of warm flesh,

burnt a rosy red beneath the hot sun. Her warmth enveloped him.

Whitaker looked down. Beneath the dress lay two dainty feet. Feet fashioned by rough hands, plaited from straw.

Wilson began work the next day. His method was a novel one. Using a long steel bar, he began to sound through the topsoil on the hill for a deep trench. A photograph, taken from the top of the steeple, assisted him in this endeavour. For a week Whitaker was aware of Wilson's slight figure, shirt sleeves rolled up, toiling under the warm sun. Where the chalk had been cut away to form a trench, an outline began to appear. As Wilson explained, this was not the result of wind erosion but rather a deliberate outline which had been filled in during the intervening centuries.

A figure began to emerge on Wilson's sketches. Over a hundred feet long and eighty feet high, the outline depicted a squat, round-faced caricature of a woman, sitting astride an animal whose identity was questionable. Wilson conjectured that it might be a dragon or a horse. A long snout or beak jutted from a narrow head. The legs were short and stumpy.

But it was the woman who fascinated Whitaker. The face, contained by a series of whirling lines, fixed his attention. Eyes that were hollow saucers peered at him from out of the past, establishing a centre of energy. The neck, hardly visible, merged into a wide trunk where two accentuated breasts spread across the horse's back. Wilson could throw no light on the identity of the figure. Its origins lay in the neolithic period, he assumed, although he could not even be certain of that. Only a full scale excavation would reveal the truth.

February turned into March. Within the space of a week, the weather, which had been unnaturally mild, deteriorated. Biting winds cut across the Morrigans. They howled round the vicarage, bringing blizzards with them. One Monday morning Whitaker rose to discover a thick white carpet covering the hills.

Wilson submitted, although reluctantly. He returned home on the Tuesday promising to resume work as soon as the weather improved. Whitaker stood on the station platform, staring up at the grey swarded sky. He regretted his companion's departure.

The snow took over a week to clear. Whitaker, confined to the vicarage for days at a stretch, found his attention drawn once again to the problem of the hill figure. He would sit in the long living room surrounded by his papers, while Mrs Annis's rubicund form flitted round him.

Increasingly, he set aside his ecclesiastical duties to delve into the identity of the hill figure. It was Mrs Annis who provided him with the clue to an apparently insoluble problem. One morning, over breakfast, she spoke in passing of Mab's Hill. At first Whitaker thought he had misheard but on questioning her further he discovered that the local people always used that name when referring to the westerly hill.

The folk name struck him as significant. Mab, Magg, Meg, what did those names signify? He recalled the reference to Macbeth's witches. In witch trials of the sixteenth century the name was frequently applied. Was there not a link with the very name of the hills, the Morrigans? He consulted a dictionary of mythology. His hunch was correct. The Morrigan was an Irish mother goddess, a great slayer of men.

But there was a further connection, a part of the jigsaw that now began to fit. His own church, St Bridget's, had been established prior to the Norman period. Whitaker was aware that when Augustine christianized Britain in the seventh century many of the older pagan ways remained and were tolerated by the priesthood. St Bridget was none other than the goddess of the great tribe of the Celtic Brigantes. A goddess of fire, her adherents lay mainly in the north of Britain.

Easter was approaching. Whitaker worked late, preparing himself for the important celebrations that lay ahead. Now he found that he was serving two masters. The strain of his duties began to tell on him. Late into the night a light burned in his study. He delved further and further into the parish records and the folklore of the surrounding countryside.

One afternoon when the clouds had vanished, he closed his books and left for the hills. For two miles he wandered along the trackway, his eyes dazzled by the broad sweep of the Hereford hills and the rolling azure above him.

On top of Mab's Hill he found a shattered sarsen and sat down, staring at the minute village beneath him. A stretch of rough turf spread round him. The soil was mostly gravel and chalk.

A crow, dotting its way between boulders, caught his eye. As he looked, he saw something gleam in the sun. Peering down where the crow had fled, he perceived a roughly hewn head jutting out of the brown mud. He knelt down and cleared away the soil that hemmed it in.

It was a small figurine, about four inches in length. The body was squat and bulbous, the legs non-existent. He stared at the small glass eyes, they caught the sun's reflection. The mud fell away easily. It was a caricature of a pregnant female. The stomach, hugely distended, was fused to the balloon-like thighs, while the cleft for the pudenda was raised and exaggerated. The eyes gleamed at him. He passed his index finger over the rounded breasts. A feeling, compounded of awe and excitement overwhelmed him.

He cleaned the figurine, wrapped it in a piece of cloth and concealed it in his trunk. He felt slightly embarrassed about the prospect of Mrs Annis seeing such a thing. Wilson replied to his letter by return of post. He was full of enthusiasm and hoped to make a return visit in April.

Right up until Maundy Thursday the Easter preparations kept Whitaker busily occupied. Every year the church committee made a tableau. It was a large affair, with wooden dolls for the soldiers and the Virgin and the crucified Christ. When finished, it stood in a niche in the Lady Chapel and attracted admiring comments from the congregation.

Good Friday was a long day for the Reverend Whitaker. Late in the evening he returned to a solitary oil lamp burning in the dining room window of the vicarage. There, between Mrs Annis's chatter and the clatter of plates, he consumed a large steak and kidney pie and three glasses of her plum wine. Normally he would have drunk a little more but he noticed a sharpness to this particular bottle which made his palate smart.

Sleep came swiftly that night. He was tired and his body ached. As he closed his eyes his mind, full of confused, disconnected images, succumbed to the fumes of the alcohol.

When he awoke it was still dark. It seemed as if he was still asleep for he could somehow see his own face, staring up into the shadow. Yet he could make out every detail in the room, even hear the tick of the travelling clock at his bedside.

One half of the room lay in profound darkness, the other was bathed in moonlight. From where he lay he could see out through the window. A bright crescent moon hung there, the horns sharp as steel.

He felt a presence in the room. Turning his head he distinguished an area of dense shadow by the door. He remembered he had hung his surplice there. But the shadow was not the shape of vestments hanging from a hook. So dark was the door that he was unable to see the outline of the oak panelling or the brass handle.

He tried to sit up in bed but was arrested by a curious lethargy. His forehead was now bathed in perspiration. Slowly, the shape by the door was shifting position, moving towards him.

He grasped the bedsheet and pulled himself upwards. A low regular breathing broke the stillness. He saw now that the shape was the figure of a woman. Her body gleamed in the reflected moonlight. There was enough light to see the long tresses of black hair falling over her shoulders. Her hips were wide, her breasts heavy.

He opened his mouth but speech was impossible. The figure glided towards him. The dark aureoles of the breasts smothered him. The sheets slipped from his hands.

The church was still cold at this hour. Daylight flooded in through the stained glass, throwing a patchwork of colours over the oak pews. He worked quickly, arranging the white altarcloth. His head ached. He had not slept well.

Beneath the pulpit a display of wild flowers surrounded a large corn dolly, plaited into the shape of a crescent moon. Noticing that it had slipped down into the foxgloves, he reached forward and put his hand between the flowers. His fingers encountered the cold stone of the pulpit. He stood staring at it for a moment. He had not really noticed the carving on the pulpit before. A band of chevron ornament ran round the outside. Beneath it was a series of roughly carved figures, each about six inches high, half obscured by luxuriant vegetation. Although badly worn, he could now see that the central figure was a naked female. The head had been almost worn away except where a triple horn hair arrangement protruded. Her right arm shot upwards, holding a long sickle. But it was that area of the body beneath the waist which fixed Whitaker's attention. The figure squatted. Between her spread legs, from a wide elongated vulva, emerged not a child but a thin sprig of vegetation.

He drew back sharply, his hand knocking over a vase of flowers.

Dusk was already falling over the Morrigan Hills. He climbed the steep footpath that led to Mab's summit. Now that evensong had ended, he felt that a great burden had been lifted from his shoulders.

Many times during that long Easter weekend he had prayed to God with the congregation and his voice had been like a thin reed against the stone walls. Up here he was free to examine his conscience. The wide spaces liberated him.

His feet followed the ancient trackway until he came to a low stile. Here he sat down and waited for darkness to fall.

In the valley beneath him St Bridget's steeple gleamed with the last dying rays of the sun. Behind him an excited flurry of birdsong presaged the approach of night.

He watched as the sky filled in like an inkblot. A chill wind passed over him. From right to left the trackway wound in an everlasting ribbon. Shapes clustered in the fields about him.

A crescent moon rose into the sky. The clean air of the countryside gave it sharp relief.

He looked down. Up the hillside, advancing at a rapid rate, came a dense oval shape, nebulous and faceless.

He stood up in alarm as the shape rushed towards him. It towered above the stile, the huge left arm circling, threatening to crush him. Black as ebony was the hand that held the scythe, black as the long tresses that swept over the shoulders and down the rippling muscles of the back . . .

The church was empty. Trembling, he pushed open the porch door, then slammed and locked it after him. For a moment he stood in the shadows, leaning against the font, breathless from exhaustion. Then he walked down the nave and sat on the altar steps.

He felt safe here. The old stones reared up about him, solid and secure. From where he sat, he could see the silver cross in the Lady Chapel, gleaming in the light of two candles.

He tried to pull himself together. In a way it was laughable. He had allowed his imagination to get the better of him. His mind was unclean. He had wandered from the path of God. He would go to the Lady Chapel. There, in the stillness of the evening, he would clear his mind and picture his Lord, risen and glorious. He crossed himself, then descended the steps. Beneath the painting of the Virgin Mother, the tableau stood, cast into relief. He peered inside. There were the figures of the mourners. About them stood the soldiers. It was a moving scene.

He looked again. Where were the figures of the Virgin and the Infant Christ? Surely no member of the congregation would have removed them?

A humped form caught his eye. He brought the candle closer. There, hidden amidst the straw, lay a crudely fashioned figure. It was grossly exaggerated, the breasts and pudenda enlarged so that they dominated the form. At its side was a long wooden club, its bulbous head shaped like a phallus.

Angrily, he picked up the figure and hurled it onto the flagstones. It shattered into pieces. He was shocked to think that anyone could contemplate such an act of sacrilege.

A sudden sound from the back of the church brought him back to his senses. He looked up. The porch door lay open. A familiar figure stood there, framed against the bell tower. He walked down the nave towards her. He was glad that she had come. Her comforting form gave him a sense of relief.

She stood behind the font, motionless, saying nothing. Normally he paid scant attention to the way she dressed but he could not fail to notice the long white dress draped over her rounded form. Her hair, usually imprisoned in a neat bun, had been let down onto her shoulders where it cascaded in a mass of curls.

'Mrs Annis . . .' he began.

Against the darkness he could see the outline of her face. It was strangely altered.

As she raised her left arm, he saw the dull blue of the blade. Still she said nothing, but when the scythe descended and cut into his neck, the image of a crescent moon rose before him. He saw the hills raised, he felt the warm flesh slipping through his fingers, then there was nothing.

Angelfish

Wendy Perriam

On three nights out of seven, Mr Chivers dreamed of purple candlewick. Sometimes, they wrapped him in it as his winding sheet; other times, it formed the fabric of the universe, and everywhere he wandered, little purple tufts tripped him up or tugged at him like burs. Occasionally, they served it up as bacon with his rubberised fried egg. He often woke screaming. He switched his torch on underneath the blankets and prayed to a purple God that Miss Lineham hadn't woken up as well. Miss Lineham slept with her door open. Maybe she didn't sleep at all, but she retired to her room at ten o'clock sharp, with a purple hairnet and a cup of cocoa and demanded silence until seven.

Mr Chivers crept out of his tangled bed into the bathroom. There it was – living, breathing candlewick – no dreamstuff, this. Purple candlewick bathmat lying exactly parallel to the cold white bath; purple candlewick toilet-seat cover, masking the shameful business that went on underneath it. Even the toilet roll was ruched and frilled in purple candlewick.

Mr Chivers stumbled over to the basin and inspected his tongue in the mirror. It was shaggy grey, as if a fine mould had settled on it in the night. His bladder was kicking him in the gut, demanding to be emptied. He hitched up his pyjama bottoms, tied the cord more tightly. He dared not risk the jet of water on white porcelain, not at 3 a.m. Even in normal daylight hours, he preferred to use the public convenience. Miss Lineham's lavatory was a decorative item. He doubted if she even used it herself. She was too refined to pee. He presumed she must evaporate off her waste-products in some

94

noiseless, odourless form of celestial dialysis. Even the cistern
was shrouded in candlewick. Miss Lineham had turned a
cesspool into an ornamental lake. Little matching doileys,
hand-crocheted in purple, smirked at him from every surface,
standing guard beneath the Harpic, cushioning the Vim. The
bathroom boasted little else. Toilet articles were strictly ban-
ned. No toothbrush was permitted to flaunt its dripping
nakedness in public; no bar of soap to wallow in its own slime.
After-shave was decadent, bathsalts an indulgence. Flannels,
toothpaste, sponges, razors – all must be locked away in
strictest purdah. In the early days, before Mr Chivers realized
the perils of exposure, he had rashly left his nail-brush by the
basin. It had seemed the sensible place for it, at the time. Miss
Lineham said nothing. But four mornings running, he found
the damply accusing object cringeing by his breakfast egg.
Four mornings running, he suffered with tension headaches
and indigestion.

Now, he never quitted the bathroom without a thorough
scrutiny. He went down on his hands and knees searching for
stray hairs or slops of water; re-positioned the bathmat dead
centre. Not that he ever dared take a bath. His feet would print
obscene naked splodges on the purple candlewick; his city dirt
might even leave a tidemark impossible to remove. The
cleaning rag was folded so squarely on the canister of Vim, it
would be sedition to disturb it.

He ran just a piddle of water into the basin. If he turned the
taps full on, the geyser roared in accusation – Miss Lineham's
private spy. He dabbed at his face, then at his private parts,
gazing upwards at the prim white ceiling, so he wouldn't get
excited. Arousal made the bed creak. He couldn't even eat an
apple in bed. The very first bite brought a warning cough from
Miss Lineham's open door. There were ways and means, of
course, if you were desperate. It was dangerous to chew, but
you could graze your teeth very gently, up and down, up and
down, against the skin, until the flesh gradually succumbed.
Then you held it in your mouth and sucked. The saliva did the
rest. It took an hour to dispose of one small Orange Pippin.
Granny Smiths were more or less impossible. Mr Chivers
stuck to Jonathans.

'I do not consider it hygienic, Mr Chivers, to store perish-
able foodstuffs among your underclothes. Nor would I have

deemed it necessary to supplement the more than adequate diet I supply.'

He couldn't even hide a Jonathan. Miss Lineham inspected everything in his room, including his underpants. She called it cleaning. She lined his cufflinks up in twos, sprayed his shoes with foot deodorant.

'Tabloid newspapers, Mr Chivers, are *not* encouraged in this establishment.'

'I have found it necessary, Mr Chivers, to invest in a new front door mat, and I should like to draw your attention to the fact.'

He never saw her smile. The nearest she got to it was at nine o'clock every other evening, when she fed her angelfish. The bevelled tank stretched its tropical turquoise luxury along a table in the hall. Jungle plants trailed soft green fingers through the water. Broad-backed leaves and ferny fronds rippled in an effervescent spume of bubbles. And through them glided the celestial colours and fairy fins of three exotic angelfish, one gold, one silver, one marbled black and cream. Their glowing opalescence seemed almost blasphemy in Miss Lineham's fawn and frowning hall. No one else in the house was indulged as were those fish. While the lodgers shivered in their fireless rooms, the angels basked in a constant eighty degrees Fahrenheit. Mr Chivers ate frugally off melamine, but the twelve varieties of vitaminised, freeze-dried fishfood lorded it on a silver tray.

Feeding time was a sacred ritual; hall lights turned low, front door locked, parlour blinds drawn down. Mr Chivers watched through a crack in his bedroom door, peering down through the banisters, awaiting that magic transformation in Miss Lineham's granite face. As the angelfish darted to the surface and nibbled at her dead white fingers, her face turned from stone to petals, the corners of her mouth lifting slightly, so that he could see the tips of plastic teeth.

'My pretty angels,' she whispered, sprinkling Magiflakes like manna. 'My pretty pretty angels.'

Mr Chivers' pulse raced. There was something about the way her cold blue eyes sparked and softened, the almost flirtatious flurry of her hand across the water. He never heard that velvet voice at any other hour; it was sackcloth and hessian when she was snapping at her lodgers.

'Some of us are born to work, Mr Chivers, and some are born to idle.'

'I do not wish Princess Margaret's name to be mentioned in this house again.'

She was even uncharacteristically generous with the fishfood. True, her angels were fed only on alternate nights, but she flung in fresh pink shrimp and bite-size worm with almost an abandon. Everyone else was rationed. Mr Chivers' scant teaspoonful of breakfast marmalade was apportioned out the evening before and sat stiffening in a plastic egg-cup overnight. He never saw the jar. Bacon rashers were cut tastefully in half. And when he had swallowed the last morsel of his one barely-buttered piece of toast (thin-sliced from a small loaf), Miss Lineham whisked every comestible swiftly out of sight. Not a crumb nor tealeaf remained to give promise of future sustenance. Even the smell of food crept cravenly away at the touch of Miss Lineham's Airfresh. Five minutes after breakfast, the kitchen looked like a morgue or a museum – shining tiles and dead exhibits in sterilized glass jars.

Mr Chivers started eating out. He sprawled in Joe's Caff or Dick's Diner, elbow-deep in chips; baked beans tumbling down his chin, wallowing in ketchup, gnawing chicken bones. ('Dogs eat bones, Mr Chivers, not Civil Service gentlemen.') He ordered both cream and custard on his syrup sponge, relished every mouthful as he slurped it down. Delirious contrast to those tight-lipped breakfasts when Miss Lineham jumped and blinked her eyes every time his teeth made contact with the toast.

He spent more and more time away. He added the public baths to the public convenience, running the bath full to overflowing and shouting above the Niagara of the taps. He set up floods and cataracts, slooshing the water over the side of the cracked white tub. He bought a plastic duck and spent reckless hours torpedoing it with the bar of municipal soap. He flung in whole cartonsful of bathsalts and turned the water as blue as Miss Lineham's fish-tank. He left hairs in the plug-hole and a rim around the bath. Nobody cared. Nobody pinned crabbed little notes on his door, saying 'Water costs money, Mr Chivers, were you aware?' No one slipped a purple crocheted doily underneath his pink soapy bottom.

He discovered a bath with a toilet beside it, for only

tenpence extra. Now he ruled the world. He jetted his urine at
the stained, un-Harpicked bowl, aiming at the central 'C' in
the maker's name, his own initial. Sometimes he took risks or
invented games, standing further and further back and still not
missing, or stopping and starting the stream, or tracing patterns with it as if the jet were a golden pencil. That done, he sat
on the cracked and germy toilet seat (which had never known
the chastening caress of candlewick) and strained and groaned
in thunderous ecstasy. He even returned to prunes.

Whatever his excesses in the Baths, he was always back in
the house by 8.55. Nine p.m. was the angels' feeding time –
the high spot of his day. Miss Lineham was often prowling by
the door.

'Good evening, Miss Lineham. Lovely weather.'

'Good evening, Mr Chivers. It won't last.'

'Good evening, Miss Lineham. Nice bit of rain for the
garden.'

'Good evening, Mr Chivers. They forecast floods.'

He rarely glanced at her. His whole attention was fixated on
the fish. He dawdled past their tank as slowly as he dared,
watching their perfect gills pant in and out, their sweepingly
dramatic ventral fins flowing like fancy ribbons from their
underbodies. There were other inhabitants of the tank, in-
elegant and drably coloured small fry, creeping things which
slimed and gobbled on the bottom, the proletariat of snail and
loach. Mr Chivers hardly noticed them – only the wide wings
and golden eyes of the angels, weaving in and out of each
other's shadows, haloed by their own enchanted fins. He
longed to know more about them, what sex they were, what
age, their parentage, their origins. He dared not ask. He dared
not even loiter by the tank. Only in his fantasy, did he lay his
cheek against the cold compress of the glass and feel his fingers
caressed by foraging mouths, the tickle of peacock tails against
his palm.

Cold reality shoved him briskly up the stairs, to cower all
evening, a prisoner in his room. He could only watch the
feeding in breathless secrecy, craning his neck, peering
through the crack, rigid with terror that Miss Lineham's eye
would swivel in its socket and meet his own. It never did. She
had eyes only for her angelfish, her concrete brow flushing and
softening as they flicked their fins and flirted with her hands.

Mr Chivers' heartbeat almost cracked the walls. He could feel his supper singing through his veins, jam on the semolina centre of his soul. This was his finale, his golden climax to a sallow day, his after-dinner port, his nuts and wine.

At 9.05 it was over. Gloom descended like a dust-sheet. Miss Lineham disappeared and was stiff and grey again by the time she re-emerged. Mr Chivers drooped in his room, dressing-gown atop his pinstripes. The one-bar fire was removed on March 1 and did not reappear until the last day of October.

'Overheating the system can be dangerous, Mr Chivers.'

'Yes, Miss Lineham.' Three inches of snow recorded at the Kew Observatory.

Mr Chivers sat and read (TV and radio were forbidden in the house). He bought every aquarist magazine on the market and squandered his Christmas bonus on a Pictorial Encyclopaedia of Tropical Fish. He turned first always to the angelfish, studied their breeding habits, learnt their Latin names. He traced their showy outlines on sheets of greaseproof paper and coloured them in with a set of Woolworth's crayons. And when at last, he fell asleep, marbled bodies and gossamer tails plunged through the spaces in his purple candlewick nightmares and turned them into gleaming silver mesh.

'SILVER JUBILEE FESTIVAL OF ANGELFISH'
April 15–21

Mr Chivers was reading in bed, his torch concealed beneath the blankets. ('Lights out at eleven, Mr Chivers. Electricity is not a gift from God.') He peered more closely at the print – a full-page advertisement in the glossy new issue of *Fishkeeper's Weekly*. Never before had so much money and attention been lavished on the species. An eccentric Yorkshire millionaire with a passion for *Pterophyllum Scalare* was sponsoring a festival in Doncaster, devoted exclusively to angelfish. Special breeds, rare specimens, unheard-of colours, generous prizes. All the local pet shops and aquaria had promised back-up displays and exhibitions for the week of the festival. Yorkshire would be awash in angelfish.

Mr Chivers had never been up North. His Easter holiday was due; he was tired of Littlehampton. He stared at the

magazine with trembling hands. He would book on Inter-
City direct to Doncaster and spend an enchanted week among
the angels.

April 22. Mr Chivers alighted at King's Cross with an empty
wallet and a suitcaseful of dirty shirts. His soul was still in
Doncaster. He jumped on the tube and plunged through rocky
clefts and tangled weed. His suburban train was packed with
angelfish. Ghostly albinos plopped between the pages of his
newspaper; aggressive all-blacks jostled his elbows and
bumped against his knees; foamy lace angels swooped past the
windows and swam along the rails. When he got off, water-
snails were clinging to his suitcase, bubbles streaming from his
nose.

He trudged from the station to the cropped and pollarded
trees of Hilldon Close. Miss Lineham met him in the hall.

'I took the liberty, Mr Chivers, of moving you to a different
room. A new gentleman lodger has arrived, who particularly
requested a location facing front.'

He jumped. Her voice had startled the rare and fantastic Liu
Keung angelfish, whom he had just persuaded to nuzzle at his
hand. 'Yes, Miss Lineham,' he muttered. He was counting the
bars on majestic marbled torsos, admiring the damask splen-
dour of stately tails.

She ushered him into a cold cramped cubicle which looked
out across the dustbins. He saw only verdant water-fern
reflecting the light from darting silver fins.

'As one of my longest-standing lodgers, Mr Chivers, I knew
I could count on your co-operation. The new gentleman is
decidedly artistic and requires a room with good light. I also
took the opportunity of replenishing your Airwick and have
added the 55p to your rent.'

'Thank you, Miss Lineham,' he murmured, as she closed
the door. He was smiling at two flirtatious silver veil-tails
rubbing noses on the ceiling. He could see their spiky back-
bones gleaming through the diaphonous silk of their flesh. He
sank smiling on the bed.

Two hours later, Doncaster was fading. Supper had been
sausages – the cheaper beef variety with a high percentage of
rusk, and mortar-mix potatoes. Mr Chivers crunched on a
lump in his custard, swilled it down with tea, returned upstairs

to the beige disapproval of his new back-room. Silver fins and
shot-silk tails had vanished, blue water leaked away, leaving
only sludge-coloured lino, purple crocheted water-lily leaves
stranded on bare wood. All his possessions had been lined up
in rows like orphans awaiting transport to an institution. His
chewing-gum was confiscated, his thirteen books (eleven of
them on fish) banished to a damp cardboard box marked 'NO
DEPOSIT, NO RETURN. LEMON BARLEY WATER'.

Mr Chivers changed into his pyjamas and sat staring at his
bunions. Miss Lineham would have thrown his feet away if he
had been rash enough to leave them in his room. Miss
Lineham liked things straight. In his jacket pocket was the
crumpled entrance ticket to the Festival. He dropped it in the
waste-bin.

Nothing left but bed. He slunk into the bathroom to clean
his teeth – stopped dead before the bath. Something was
different, dangerous. He glanced around. The toilet seat was
up! In all his years at Miss Lineham's, it had never been left up.
If some new inmate in his raw foolishness forgot to replace the
cover, Miss Lineham would dart into the bathroom after him
and snap it shut. Four or five repeats and the trembling tenant
was completely cured. Candlewick became part of defecation.

The same with toiletries. An untrained lodger's first few
breakfasts were often egg-and-flannel or sausage-and-loofah,
the table littered with hang-dog razors and confiscated shaving
sticks. Cure was always swift. Or had been up till now. Mr
New-Boy Gordon had been in residence a week, so what was
his orange flannel doing draped across the bath – flagrant,
dripping, not even folded . . . ? Miss Lineham was at home,
so why had she not removed this blushing flag of revolution?
Why had no contemptuous note been pushed beneath the
offender's door? As far as he could ascertain, she was still in her
right mind. Or had been so at supper.

'Since you appear to be having so much difficulty in dispos-
ing of your second sausage, Mr Chivers, I shall apportion it to
Mr Gordon in future.'

He saw the offending sausage, wreathed in Coleman's
mustard and Miss Lineham's smiles. She never smiled. Chivers clutched at the basin for support. How could he have been
so blind? The new Artistic Gentleman had changed her,
softened her, found the flinty remnants of her heart and

swathed them in his shameless orange flannel. An upstart, a
greenhorn, stinking out the house with aftershave, taking
artistic licence with the purple candlewick . . .

Mr Chivers strode back to his room, stared in fury at the
stag at bay. One picture per room. 'Nothing, I repeat nothing,
is to be stuck or pinned onto lodgers' bedroom walls.' He
hated stags – all their vaunting headgear. It had been a Victorian flower-girl in his previous room – tyro Gordon's room –
with nothing on her head but blonde curls and a circlet of
roses, a froth of white pantaloons teasing beneath her skirt.

He opened his wardrobe and stared at his row of ties, all
limp, all drably coloured. He took out a bar of Cadbury's
Wholenut chocolate, hidden in a slipper, put it back again.
Wholenut was the riskiest confection on the market. If you bit
into a hazelnut, it made a crack to wake the dead. And Miss
Lineham was very much alive. He had noticed it at supper. She
had hovered over Mr Gordon all through the bread-and-
butter pudding, offering him Jersey cream from a silver jug.
Melamine and custard had always been the rule.

He could hear her now, her brown no-nonsense lace-ups
phat-phatting from kitchen to hall. Mr Chivers sprang up
from his chair. Feeding time! Every other night at Doncaster
he had tuned in, in mind and spirit, to that magic ritual,
hearing Miss Lineham's fin-enchanted voice winging after
him on Inter-City. 'My pretty angels, my pretty pretty
angels.'

He crept to his bedroom door and opened it a crack.
Useless. His new room was stuck away around a corner. He
was cut off, shut out, excluded from those holy rites. No
longer could he peer down through the banisters and share
the azure mysteries of the tank. He heard the brogues shuffle to
a stop, and then the sound of voices. Voices? He slunk out of
his room onto the landing; could see only squiggled lino and
stripey wall. His full-frontal view of the hall had departed with
the roses and the pantaloons. He tiptoed along the passage,
round the corner to the top of the stairs. Peered down. Miss
Lineham was there, the flushed-and-radiant-feeding-time-
Miss Lineham, lingering almost coquettishly by the tank.
But she was not alone. Standing beside her, almost leaning
against her, was Mr Basil A. F. Gordon; black eyes, white
hands, topiary moustache. Four eyes staring at the fish, four

hands trailing in the torrid water, two heads almost joined as one.

The largest angelfish was nibbling at Mr Gordon's index finger. Chivers could feel the throb and tingle in his own. The new Artistic Gentleman was making stylish patterns with rose-coloured shrimp flakes on turquoise water. All three angels swooped to the surface and kissed his hand. Mr Chivers' palms vibrated with the tiny pressure of their worshipping mouths. Miss Lineham was pointing at a fin. He could hear the husky murmur of her voice, confiding those intimate details she had always denied to him – the personal histories of the angelfish, their weaknesses, their gender, their little fads and foibles. He could see her own pale mouth opening and shutting almost in time with theirs, the flush on her opalescent skin, her strange gold eyes.

'My pretty angels,' she was murmuring. 'My pretty pretty angels.' But it was Basil Gordon she was turned towards.

'May I help you, sir?' inquired the salesman.

'Yes,' said Mr Chivers. 'I want three angelfish. One gold, one silver, one marbled black and cream.'

'Certainly, sir.' The salesman led him over to the corner. The fish were smaller than Miss Lineham's.

'Don't worry, sir; they'll grow to fit the tank.' He made a little flurry with his net. 'You'll be wanting a tank as well, I presume?'

Mr Chivers shook his head.

'You've *got* a tank? Right, how about a heater? Or a piston pump? Or an under-gravel filter unit?'

'No,' said Mr Chivers. 'Thank you.'

'All right for fishfood, are you?'

'I won't be needing food.'

'Growlux lighting? Stimulates plant life. Choice of pink or blue.'

'Just the fish,' repeated Mr Chivers.

He carried them on the bus in a polythene bag fastened with a rubber band, his capacious sponge-bag in the other hand. People stared.

'Not so bright this morning, is it?' remarked the woman at the Public Baths who issued him his ticket and his towels.

He didn't answer. He needed all his concentration to conceal

the bag of fish beneath his raincoat. His usual cubicle was free.
He double-locked the door, slipped the polythene bag into the
basin. He didn't release the angels; time enough for that. He
ran his bath, tipping in almost half a bottle of Blue-Mist Foam,
so that azure bubbles frothed above the sides. He unwrapped
his plastic duck, littered the floor with sponges, brushes,
flannels, then turned back to the angelfish, wrenching off the
rubber band, tossing the bag on the floor. It landed on its side,
jarring the writhing bodies. Slowly, the water leaked away.
The fishes flowed out with it, marooned and slithering on the
shiny tiles. The gold angel twitched and palpitated, leaping six
inches in the air then somersaulting down again with a sickening thud. Mr Chivers paused a moment to admire the markings on the marbled angel, almost identical to Miss Lineham's
specimen. Its mouth was opening and shutting in a wordless
plea, its feeble tail flailing on the tiles.

Chivers climbed into the bath. The water was armpit high.
He could hear the overflow gurgling down the pipe. He picked
up a sponge and slapped his thighs with it. He stuck a crooked
foot through a tower of foam. There were so many bubbles
you could lose whole limbs. Steam was rising from the water,
falling again in streams of condensation down the walls. He
leaned over the edge of the tub and saw the silver angelfish
plunging and zigzagging in a frenzied attempt to reach the
water, its gills pistoning in and out in panic, its eyes almost
starting from its head.

Mr Chivers began to sing. The marbled angel had fallen into
a drain-hole and was floundering on its back. Mr Chivers
loofahed his upper arms. The soap was lost and melting at the
bottom of the tub. He stretched and yawned in the benison of
steam. He could see the fishes through his half-closed eyes, the
marbled angel growing feebler now. Its mouth gaped open, as
if it had been unhinged. Its eyes were glazing over.

Chivers ran more water, laughing aloud as the hoarse hot
tap thundered between his feet. Every time he moved, the
bubbles frothed and flurried over the sides. He turned on his
belly and lost his chin in foam. The silver angel was only a pale
splodge on the tiles. Its eyes were still open, but the gills were
shuttered and inert. The gold angel kept on fighting. Its leaps
were lower now, but it still struggled to save itself, panting
and throbbing with each agonised contortion. Mr Chivers

wallowed in his tub, rocking backwards and forwards on his bottom, so that the water sloshed and seesawed from one end to the other. Bubbles were pricking and popping all along his limbs; a soft pink flush pyjamaed him from brow to bunions. When he sang, the words resounded off the walls, adding a choir and organ to his voice.

The brave gold angel was singing along with him. He could see its mouth gasping open, wheezing out the words, its once-majestic tail trailing like a broken rudder. The other two fish were motionless. Only their eyes stared upwards, as if they were praying for deliverance.

Chivers pulled out the plug, listening to the water chuckle down the waste-pipe. He stepped out onto the tiles, careful to avoid the corpses, dried himself on stiff municipal towels, then flung them wet and soggy in a corner. He picked up the three small bodies and placed them in the toilet bowl. They floated on the top, their colours still unfaded, their eyes beseeching. There was a flicker of life in the golden angel still. It twitched in shock as it felt itself fall on water. Slowly, it spread its tail, jerked its fins, struggled between triumph and extinction. Mr Chivers stood above it, legs astride. He watched the jet of golden urine strike and shatter it. Three broken bodies whirled and plummeted in their porcelain goldfish bowl, colliding with each other as the gilded waterfall spewed on.

'My pretty angels,' he murmured, as he traced an 'L' with the last slowing dribble. 'My pretty pretty angels.' He pulled the chain and watched them churn and rupture down the bend.

He was humming as he trudged back to his lodgings, his hair slicked down, his shoes high-shined with a wad of toilet paper. The nail-brushes were dried, the flannels folded, the plastic duck caged safely in its sponge-bag. Miss Lineham had never approved of toys.

She met him at the front door. His quiet grey raincoat was neatly belted, his nails were double-scrubbed with coal tar. A spruce white handkerchief burst into late-spring flower from his top right pocket.

'Good evening, Miss Lineham. It looks like a storm.'

'Good evening, Mr Chivers. I'm afraid you're wrong. The barometer is rising. Set Fair it says and Set Fair it's going to be. Now, will you kindly go upstairs and wash your hands. I am serving supper early. Mr Gordon has most kindly invited me to see his Exhibition and I don't wish to be late.'

Mr Chivers paused by the fish-tank. The golden angel was spiralling lazily towards him, flaunting its outrageous tail, gills throbbing, mouth insolently open. He could see its topaz eyes smiling at him, smiling . . . He turned away.

'Yes, Miss Lineham,' he whispered. And went upstairs.

Poor Edith

Eugenie Hill

'Why is that little boy making all that noise?' Isabel asked, observing a purple-faced infant being dragged along as she and her grandmother were on the way to the station after an early lunch.

'I'm sure I don't know,' her grandmother said absently. 'I suppose he wants sweets or something.'

'He won't get them any quicker for shouting,' Isabel observed. Her eyes widened in shock. 'He's just bitten his mother! Now he's kicking her leg. She's *very* cross. He's a naughty little boy, isn't he, Granny?'

Receiving the assurance that he was indeed very naughty she felt a small frisson of satisfaction. The world was gratifyingly full of such children, a fact which greatly enhanced Isabel's own reputation for irreproachable behaviour.

They caught the train with six minutes to spare. In the compartment Isabel faced her grandmother, her hands folded on top of her blue leather handbag, her feet in highly polished black shoes not quite touching the floor. She was wearing a smart coat of blue-flecked tweed with blue velvet trimming on the collar. Her dark eyes peered out alertly from beneath her neat cap of black hair.

'It won't rain, will it, Granny?' she asked as the train pulled out of the station and a bright but cloud-studded sky was revealed.

Her grandmother, comfortably knitting, said she doubted it.

'Because I don't want Edith to get wet when I'm wheeling

her, you know.' Isabel fingered the grain of the leather hand-bag. 'So it had just better keep fine, hadn't it?'

Although she had not yet seen her, Isabel had heard about Edith often in her short life. Edith and her grandmother had been best friends when they were both little girls themselves, more than fifty years ago, but Edith had been the unlucky one. A serious illness had deprived her completely of the use of her legs.

'Why didn't the doctors make her better?' Round-eyed Isabel had complete faith in the medical profession. 'Why didn't they take her to the hospital and make her legs well again?'

They had tried everything, she was told, but it was useless. Edith never walked again.

'They called it infantile paralysis, though the proper name for it is poliomyelitis. Many children who caught it were left crippled,' Isabel's grandmother explained vaguely. 'Fortunately it's very rare now because of injections and things. In our time, of course, there was nothing of that sort. It simply had to be accepted.'

'Poor Edith,' Isabel murmured compassionately. She thought she would say 'infantile paralysis' and 'poliomyelitis' over and over to herself until she knew them by heart and could astound people by her cleverness.

She was hastily assured, lest the story should alarm her too much, that the tragedy hadn't broken Edith. She was a wonderful, wonderful person, sleeping in the downstairs sitting-room and going out in an invalid chair. She had remained Isabel's grandmother's best friend through all the years of the latter's marriage and beyond. She was uncom-plaining, unselfish, vivacious. Her cheerful letters were an inspiration. She thought the world of Isabel's mother, had cried with happiness when she saw her in her wedding dress, had cried again on hearing of the birth of Isabel, and kept a picture of the baby when only three days old on permanent display on her piano.

Now Isabel had come to stay on her own for a month at her grandmother's house and she was at last being taken to meet Edith. They would have tea and she would be shown the picture of herself only three days old. Then, providing it kept fine, they would take Edith to a nearby park to feed the ducks and Isabel was going to be allowed to push the invalid chair.

It was this last fact, so casually advanced, which really captivated her. She had always wanted to wheel a real live baby out in a pram and the idea of pushing a grown-up person was so much more novel that it took her breath away.

She rehearsed beforehand by fishing out her own old push chair from the garden shed. She wrapped her grandmother's indolent tabby cat in her doll's shawl, explained to him that he had lost the use of his legs, and wheeled him round the front of the house and out into the avenue.

The outing was not a success however. The foolish creature kept complaining and sliding about and at last, impatient at his own former acquiescence, he leapt down and ran awkwardly away, trailing the shawl in a muddy puddle. It didn't matter really, Isabel assured herself philosophically she'd be doing the real thing soon enough.

The train journey took thirty-five minutes, during which time she was pleasingly aware of the approval of the other occupants of their carriage. A gentleman in a brown suit smiled at her covertly from behind his newspaper and wiggled his ears and his bristly moustache. Isabel knew that this was done for her entertainment alone since no one else could see his face. A lady opposite offered her a fruit pastille and her grandmother signalled that it was all right to accept it.

'There'll be *lots* and *lots* of time for wheeling Edith out after tea,' she said, settling the bulge of the pastille contentedly in her cheek. 'And I *will* push her all by myself, won't I, Granny?'

As soon as they emerged from the station of the town where Edith lived, they went into a florist's shop. There, Isabel's grandmother selected primroses and violets. The assistant made them up into a round posy and wrapped them in pink paper and tied a purple ribbon round them.

'You shall carry these, Isabel,' her grandmother said munificently. 'Hand them to Edith the moment we arrive. Flowers mean so much to her.'

She approached a taxi and informed the driver crisply that they wanted to go to Beech Avenue, number fifteen.

'Right you are, missus,' he said jauntily, tossing aside the paperback he was reading and winking at Isabel.

She thought she had never seen anything so pretty as the

little posy. She sat in the back of the taxi wafting it under her
nose until she could almost taste the violets' perfume.

The road in which they were deposited was lined with large
old trees just coming into leaf. A row of neat, semi-detached
houses faced the promised park. Soon, soon, Isabel reminded
herself with a surge of joy as her grandmother paid the
taxi-driver, she herself would be in that park wheeling Edith in
her chair.

Edith's house had a high privet hedge and a yellow painted
gate with the number fifteen on it. Isabel's excitement
mounted as she followed her brisk grandmother up a short,
flagged path to a front door of frosted glass.

'That's new, of course,' her grandmother commented. 'The
door was wooden when I was young. Edith had it replaced
about ten years ago.'

Isabel meant to ask if she might press the bell push but her
grandmother's finger was already on it and they could hear
melodious chimes sounding faintly from within the house.

Isabel, her face alight with anticipation, adjusted the handbag on her left arm and raised the pretty posy in her right hand,
catching as she did the violets' scent.

They waited for what seemed a long time. A bunchy white
cloud passed momentarily in front of the sun, in the road a car
rumbled by. From the depths of the house there came at last a
faint shuffling which grew gradually into a dragging sound.
Isabel's smile faded a little. For the first time she was touched
by a slight unease.

Through the opacity of the glass something undefinable
could be seen slowly approaching. It was low to the ground. It
crawled. Isabel's stomach gave a great sick swoop as an
amorphous shape loomed up and a horribly distorted face was
pressed against the glass.

She did not see, as the door swung open, the little, eager-
faced woman on the paisley-patterned carpet with the thin
hands reaching outward and upward and the useless legs
trailing. What Isabel saw was something unspeakable, product
of frosted glass and of her own imagination. It filled her with a
panic, black, unreasoning and total.

With a convulsive jerk accompanied by a strange, whin-
nying sound she fled down the path. She dropped the posy
which split as it hit the flags, spattering violets and primroses,

pink paper and purple ribbon everywhere. Oblivious of the
startled voice of her grandmother calling out her name Isabel
ran with her head down through the yellow gate and out onto
the pavement. She hurtled across the road with no thought of
the painstakingly learned Green Cross Code and blundered
blindly through tall iron gates.

Once inside the park she continued to run instinctively, her
mind devoid of concrete thoughts. She twisted and turned,
crossed open grass, skirted a pond where ducks and toy boats
bobbed, and disappeared into a clump of bushes. There, as if
some mechanism controlling her had run down, she slowed to
a halt, shaking and sobbing, on a narrow, shrub-screened
path.

Gradually she became aware of the sounds of normality; an
electric grass cutter, the shrill cries of distant children. She
rubbed a hand smelling faintly of violets across her face and
discovered that her cheeks were damp.

Her handbag was still clamped tightly against her left side.
Upon opening it she was immediately comforted by the glint
of the gold case of an old lipstick, rescued after her mother
had discarded it, and by a glimpse of an ornamental perfume
bottle filled with coloured water which had been similarly
acquired.

Her breath shuddered as she scrabbled for a handkerchief
with a rabbit motif in the corner. Despite the reassurance the
sight of familiar possessions brought, she felt a hollowness
inside. Babyishly she longed for the continued anaesthetizing
solace of her own tears but investigative sniffs and sighs
proved that she had cried herself out.

She was standing on the shady path with no thought of what
she would do next when she became aware of something
damp and cool pressing against her bare leg. As she glanced
down her eyes met the serious gaze of a fat black dog of the
Labrador type. She extended her fingers cautiously and a
moist, quivering nose attentively examined them. A broad
pink ribbon of tongue, unrolling, tasted them speculatively
one by one.

'Hey up there, Prince! What you up to now? Steady on, old
lad!'

The man who rounded the corner wore a cloth cap above a
seamed, yellow face.

'Don't be afeared.' His voice, low and husky, seemed to wheeze up effortfully from some deep recess beyond his throat. 'He'll not hurt you. Soft as a babby, is our Prince.'

The dog looked back at him and wagged a thick tail so vigorously that the whole of his broad rear wobbled as if in confirmation.

'Does Prince like little girls?' Isabel asked, testing the name cautiously.

'Aye, he does that! Always one for the lasses, eh, Prince?' Stooping, he tickled the dog behind the ears. 'He lets Tracy, that's my daughter's youngest, ride round the kitchen on his back.'

Isabel, charmed by the anecdote, asked the age of this fortunate girl.

'There you've got me. Memory's not what it were.' He shifted his cap to scratch his head. 'Let's see now. She must be all of two and a half, seeing as her birthday was last October.'

'I'm five and three-quarters,' volunteered Isabel with a faintly superior smile but it was with anxiety that she added, 'Is Tracy a good little girl?'

'She'll do. And how about you?'

Isabel felt a stab of pain.

'I'm good nearly always,' she said defensively. '*Mostly* I'm a very good girl.'

She blinked back tears which unaccountably started in her eyes.

'I'm sure of that,' the man said kindly. He stared at her with a puzzled air. 'Come to the park with your mammy did you, love?'

'I came with Granny. On the train. We were going to see someone.' Isabel looked up into his uncensuring face. 'I ran away,' she admitted flatly.

'From your grandmother?' At her reluctant nod his bushy eyebrows disappeared into the shade of his cap's peak. 'How's that? You'll be wanting to look for her.'

Isabel shook her head. The corners of her mouth drooped. Compulsively she clicked the clasp of her handbag. Aware that at any minute she might cry again, she fixed her concentration firmly on the dog which had flopped panting onto the path. The skin around his mouth was soft and grey and a few

stubby white hairs poked through it. His nose, damp at the tip,
was cracked and dry and lumpy further up.

'Prince looks awfully old,' she said.

'Thirteen come July,' the master confirmed.

Isabel put out her small hand and the tail started up in
automatic response. Gravely she patted the lumpy head.
Carefully she stroked the broad back, flattening the hair from
the nape of his thick neck to his rump as she did with the fur of
the cat in her grandmother's house.

'He can stand a lot of that,' the man said, smiling.

'He's a very good dog, isn't he?'

It was confirmed that Prince had given no one a day's
trouble in his life. Isabel sighed.

The fluffy white clouds had moved away from the sun and
the path was flooded with warm light. Gently Isabel touched
the recumbent Prince's underside. Like the skin around his lips
it was greyish there and slightly palpitating.

'Can you remember where you were when you lost sight of
your grandma?' the man asked casually.

'Oh, yes. It was outside her friend's house. Miss Edith
Schofield, fifteen Beech Avenue.' Isabel began by reeling
off the words with her old confidence then, remembering,
stumbled at the end.

'Beech Avenue's on the other side of the park. You've come
a fair way. Your grandma will be searching all over for you,'
he said, adding, since she only stroked Prince more fiercely,
'Happen we'd best go and find her now, eh?'

Doubtfully Isabel considered.

'I wouldn't mind so long as Prince came,' she said at last.

'Try and stop him!' the man said heartily. 'Our best road is
to cut across by the pond. On your way, lad!'

He moved as slowly as he spoke and Isabel found it easy to
keep pace with him.

'Do you have a lead for Prince?' she asked, checking that the
dog was following at their heels.

'There'll be one in the house somewhere, I suppose. Never
use it myself. Prince is not one for running off.'

Isabel slipped her hand into his. The palm was rough and
warm. Ducks quacked at them as they passed the pond
chatting easily together. It seemed that Prince's master had
been a miner all his life. He told of a dim, subterranean world

of rattling waggons and toiling ponies. But for five years now
he had been unable to work because of coal dust settled on his
chest. He coughed to illustrate the terrible effects of this.

In return Isabel told of her father's job and of how it took
him to many different parts of the world. She explained that
her mother was at that moment in the Middle East with him,
which was why she was staying at her grandmother's house.
She spoke at some length of the cat's shortcomings as a
playmate. She revealed no details of the events of the afternoon.

Walking and talking thus she decided that it would suit her
very well to stay here. She would live with this old man and
play with Tracy, teaching her many things. Prince's lead
would soon be found and she would be able to bring him to the
park every day. She longed to take out dogs on leads. Her
father said it wouldn't be fair to have one of their own, since he
moved about so much.

As they came to the main gates of the park she saw her
grandmother approaching in the company of a man in a
navy-blue uniform. Upon seeing Isabel she exclaimed and
darted forward. She looked hot and cross and her hat was
slightly askew.

'You naughty girl, wherever have you *been*?' she cried,
seizing Isabel's arm with unaccustomed roughness. 'I've been
looking all over for you. Whatever possessed you, running off
like that?'

She looked very sharply at Prince's master. Dark suspicions
chased one another across her eyes. But it seemed that the park
keeper knew him. Already the two men were talking amiably
together in their broad, slow voices.

'Little lass gave herself some sort of a fright.'

'No harm done, though.'

'You'll be right as rain now you've found your grandma,
eh, love?'

Isabel's grandmother at once became gracious. The manner
in which she expressed her gratitude to Prince's master was
regal. Firmly she commanded Isabel to thank him for all his
trouble. At last, showering final effusions, she pulled Isabel
away, a warm smile still affixed to her face. The two men
raised their caps then moved off in the direction of the bowling
green with the dog waddling in their wake.

As soon as they were alone Isabel's grandmother wiped her face clean of the social smile.

'Silly girl! You gave poor Edith a terrible fright. What *have* you done to your face? It's filthy.'

Outside the park gates Isabel was ordered to spit on a tissue. Her cheeks were ruthlessly scrubbed so that they reddened and stung.

'Come along now,' her grandmother said severely, moving on so quickly that Isabel had to trot to keep up. 'No more nonsense.'

Yet when they had crossed the road and stood once more before the yellow gate, Isabel proved unexpectedly defiant. She would not go in, she said, she no longer wanted to see Edith. She wanted to go home.

There ensued one of those futile and protracted arguments in which she had often seen other people's children engaged and which she had so much deplored. But her face was peculiarly stiff and set. Her bewildered grandmother found her unshakeable.

'Won't you at least come in for a moment, just to say goodbye to Edith?' she asked at last dispiritedly.

Their previous relationship had given her no preparation for such a confrontation with the child and all the harassment and standing about in the road had tired her. She looked elderly and anxious.

Isabel shook her head emphatically.

'Must I go in by myself then?' her grandmother rather piteously asked. 'Very well. You'd better stand inside the gate.' With a resigned expression she clicked the latch behind them. 'But don't you dare go wandering off again.'

'No, Granny,' said Isabel, meek in her victory.

Her grandmother's feet, neat in broad fitting beige court shoes, clicked aggrievedly on the flags. The front door was ajar. She passed inside, closing it behind her.

Isabel waited beside the privet hedge. She was warm inside her coat. In the distance a woman laughed. Someone must have taken in the violets and primroses. There was no sign of them on the path. She pulled a privet leaf for the satisfaction of the crack it gave when folded over.

As long as she kept her eyes firmly averted from the frosted glass of the front door she felt no alarm. She opened her handbag and took out the ornamental perfume bottle, wrinkling her nose to catch some vestige of scent. Dreamily she thought of Prince, the gloss on his back where the sun struck it. She pictured herself walking past the duck pond with him on a lead.

When at last the door opened again she sprang back, fearful that a little crippled woman would be revealed, dragging herself over the threshold, scuttling down the path with claw-like hands reaching out.

But Isabel's grandmother was alone. She shut the door behind her in a final way and took Isabel's hand and they returned in silence to the railway station. It seemed fitting that this time there should be no wiggling ears, no fruit pastilles. The train was almost empty.

They arrived home much earlier than had been intended and ate a dull tea in silence. It was only much later when Isabel was in bed and her grandmother stooping to kiss her goodnight that she exclaimed suddenly,

'What a funny little girl! Fancy being frightened of poor Edith. It was a bit silly, wasn't it?'

Isabel said nothing.

For the remainder of her stay she was her customary, tractable self. It seemed she had developed an aversion to her old push chair. Instead of wheeling the cat out in it she attached a length of string to his flea collar and tried ineffectually to persuade him to go for walks with her.

Her grandmother did not refer again to the abortive outing until Isabel's mother came. Then she spoke low and rapidly so that only isolated snatches of what she said reached Isabel, playing with her doll in a corner of the room.

'. . . you know she loves opening the door to her visitors *herself* . . . must have been some reflection through the glass . . . right out into the road, so dangerous . . . a miner, awfully decent sort of person, *fortunately*,' as the recollections tumbled out an aggrieved note crept in, '. . . *refused* to go back in . . . beautiful tea all laid . . . disappointment for the poor soul . . . never have believed the child could be like that . . .'

Isabel's mother listened indulgently, patting shining dark hair, yawning discreetly behind a manicured hand.

'Children get these odd notions, Mother. Isabel's an imaginative little thing. Never you mind, poppet,' she raised her voice. 'You and I will go and see Edith together one of these days. It'll be all right next time.'

She smiled, radiant with her own beauty and bounty while her mother sniffed and clicked knitting needles.

But Isabel knew it could never be all right. There was an area of pleasure closed now to Edith and to herself. However much she might have liked to be able to love her grandmother's friend, her horror of the scuttling, creeping, formless thing behind the frosted glass left no room for compassion.

'Prince was thirteen,' she said softly, smoothing down her doll's dress. 'That's very old for a big dog.' The two women stared at her uncomprehendingly as, her voice gathering strength, she went on in a tone in which defiance and love and loss were inextricably mingled. 'And he liked me, Prince did. Prince liked me a *lot*.'

A New Dawn

Mary Foulkes

When it was nearly light a dog started barking at the other side of the settlement. It was a harsh urgent sound and people stirred in their beds and some of them got up and went outside to see what was happening. In his own shack Lucas lay thinking about how this small incident underlined the difference between the present and the past. Once, long ago, a dog barking in the dawn would have been a nuisance. He would have grumbled to his wife about it and made a note to speak to his neighbour later. Now it could mean anything or nothing. He hoped the dog was simply restless, perhaps there was a bitch in heat he had scented. Perhaps, on the other hand, there was real danger.

Lucas stayed in bed, lying fairly comfortably on his worn mattress, covered by one much mended blanket and a couple of home cured sheepskins. He was a camp elder now. He could let the youngsters investigate. His bedroom was one of the two rooms in the shack and at this time of year, early spring, it was damp and cold. The glass had gone in the window some years ago and he had filled it in until it was a narrow slit and hung an old sack over it to keep out the draughts. Now a little light slid in round the edges of this and shone faintly on the rough stones of the wall.

The dog was still barking and voices were beginning to murmur outside. Lucas sat up reluctantly and reached for his sheepskin poncho which he put on over his worn woollen garments, still sitting in the bed with the blanket drawn up around his knees. It was still the double bed they had bought when they were first married and dragged up the hill after the new life had begun. Now he had it to himself since Lisa had died in November. These cheerless winters had always been hardest on her and for the last weeks of her life she had stayed in the bed, shivering under the covers while he warmed old bricks in the embers and put them in next to her, wrapped in rags. He still associated that time with the smell of scorching. Later on, as the days darkened and shortened, she had turned away from him and lay facing the wall, her knees drawn up towards her chest and her arms wrapped around them. She hardly ever spoke to him then and almost stopped eating. He coaxed her to drink a little warm milk from time to time. Once she grumbled, saying she would have preferred it sweetened, but their sugar had been used up long before. One dark morning he had woken up and touched her and found she was quite cold. One of the younger men had helped him to dig the grave. Every winter some more of the older people died. They missed the comforts of the old days and the medicines and medical care that would otherwise have kept them going. Some of them looked very strange with their thin grey hair straggling over their shoulders, their sunken toothless mouths and thin sinewy arms and legs. Dental treatment, or the lack of it, had become a real problem and many people suffered agonizing pain from decaying teeth. The youngest were the best off. They had never had sugar in their diet and it helped. In other ways they were not so lucky. In such a small isolated group the effects of interbreeding showed clearly and quite a few of the youngsters were retarded, or just a little dull or slow. In their present way of life it did not really matter, in fact they were well adapted to it. Lucas sometimes wondered if they were the new men who would inherit the new world.

He got up now and moved stiffly into the next room. Here in one corner next to the hearth an electric cooker gleamed against the wall. A food processor stood on top of it, unusable for many years. Lisa had kept both dusted and sometimes put a jar of flowers there too. She had always insisted that one day they might work again. She had used her blackened pots over the wood fire reluctantly and sometimes stood sadly in front of the cooker turning the knobs on and off and adjusting the thermostat. Lucas poked a few twigs into the heart of the smouldering fire, balanced a kettle on top and went out into the strengthening light.

He stood just outside looking around. Other people were coming out too and one or two figures crouched on the low embankment that encircled the settlement. At one point there was a gap in this defensive wall and there more people were gathered. Lucas set off to join them. Long before history was properly recorded, this place had been a hilltop fort, and before the disaster had come, Lucas and the others who sheltered here now had lived in a village at the foot of the hill. When the danger had threatened them and they were still able to listen to news bulletins on the radio, they had been advised to get as high as possible and they had climbed up to the great embankment and built their new village inside it, dragging as much as they could up from their old homes and bringing sheep and cattle with them. How many years ago had that been, Lucas wondered now. He hardly knew any more but he had been a young man then and Lisa was still a pretty girl.

The dog had stopped barking at last and birds were singing strongly all around. He reached the gap and looked down the slope and out across the low ground to the north. Now that there were no more cars, farming or building, the scrub had begun to take over the landscape, creeping over the fields until it was hard to see where the hedges had been. Five miles away a motorway had once passed, joining London to the west. Now there was a continuous line where it had run, a break in the vegetation, but that was all. Everything below was peaceful, unpolluted, untouched for many years. Only their own sheep and cattle grazed close to them on the slopes. So far as they could see there was nothing else moving apart from the birds.

'How beautiful,' a voice murmured and Lucas saw Muriel standing just below him beyond the gap. She was one of the best adjusted of the older ones and delighted in their lack of sophisticated comforts. In the old days she had lived in a commune, growing vegetables and looking after rabbits and hens. She had had long hair and long skirts that trailed in the grass. She had smoked pot and written poems. Now she did much the same except that the pot had all gone long ago in spite of her efforts to grow it from seed. She had put herself in charge of the rabbits, which were kept in pens at the back of the enclosure. Here they multiplied themselves busily and here dogs were tethered to keep the wild foxes at bay. But the biggest problem was keeping the rabbits in rather than the foxes out. From many years in the open air her face and arms were like polished leather and her hair though grey was still long and thick. She was perfectly well and perfectly happy, living in what she thought of as a perfect world.

'Just smell this air,' she said now, 'and listen to those larks.' She tilted her face towards the sky, shutting her eyes and spreading her hands out towards the sun. All around her men and women peered anxiously down the slope but she stood relaxed, breathing deeply, her bare feet planted firmly in the mud.

'Perhaps it was a fox,' Lucas said to the young man next to him, who stood with a heavy stick ready in his hand. He turned for a moment and said slowly, 'He wouldn't bark like that for a fox. Not on and on like that. He's used to foxes. He knows them. He might bark for another dog, but not a fox. He's used to foxes.' He shifted the stick and looked off into the scrub uneasily. He was one of the slower ones, not quite retarded, but not so quick as he should be. The dog had never barked for so long before and the whole concept it presented was strange to him. He could not cope with it.

'After all,' Lucas said, 'it's not likely we would be the only ones to survive, it might be people or some big animal.' He thought vaguely of zoos and animals escaping through the rusted wire.

'People,' the young man said patiently as if speaking to a child. 'We are people.' He waved his hand towards the settlement as if that was the end of the subject.

Lucas looked from his dull puzzled face to Muriel's, still blindly ecstatic and tilted upwards. He touched her arm. 'I put the kettle on before I came out,' he said. 'Come back and have some tea. Nothing's happening here. They'll keep watch anyway.'

'Tea,' she said opening her eyes. 'Indian or China?' She cackled suddenly and turned away from the hillside. 'Bramble leaves,' he said sombrely.

In the living room she wrenched the oven door open, saying 'What do you keep in this thing anyway?' A heap of ancient womens' magazines fell out, all faded to a brittle yellow brown. 'Poor Lisa,' she said, 'she always clung to the past.' She picked the papers up and pushed them back where they came from. 'Dreadful things,' she said. 'What a false picture

they gave of women – and gave women of themselves – what's
worse. Poor prettified little things, making their faces up and
waiting for their husbands to come home for supper.' She sat
down heavily in the worn-out armchair and sank until she was
almost resting on the floor, with her knees high in front of her.
Under the edge of her tattered skirt her big bare toes poked out
towards the fire. Lucas handed her a mug of tea and sat down
himself.

'Do you really think there could be other people out there?'
she said. Lucas sighed. This question had been a constant
subject of discussion between the older people, taking over
from their earlier preoccupation – could there be life on other
planets?

'I can't believe we are the only survivors,' he said now.
'Some freak of weather or geography saved us. There must
have been others in a similar situation.'

Muriel relaxed as far as she could in the old chair. The steam
from the tea drifted up in front of her face and she looked
through it dreamily at him. 'Why do we always see it as a
threat, I wonder,' she said. 'It could be a good thing to have
more of us. We could get together, pool our resources, share
tools . . .'

'Let's hope so,' said Lucas, 'we just can't know. They might
be criminals, they might be clergymen. How can we tell? The
last thing we want is to land ourselves in tribal disputes, but
I'm afraid it would happen. Our youngsters have no idea of
living with outsiders.'

'Some of them have no ideas at all,' Muriel said sharply. 'If
someone new doesn't come along soon we will have degener-
ated into a collection of morons.'

'You're exaggerating as usual,' Lucas said and turned away
to put another log on the fire. His stomach rumbled and
he remembered that he had had no breakfast yet. He usually
made himself a watery soup flavoured with wild herbs and
thickened with potato. He supposed he would have to invite
Muriel to share it. 'No,' she said, she had eaten before she
came out.

'Do you ever think of the breakfasts we used to have?' she
asked, watching him heat his soup over the fire.

'Well, we still have eggs,' he said, trying not to sound dis-
contented.

'I suppose you must miss Lisa a lot.' She was determined to be sorry for him.

'She never liked it here,' he said briefly.

He poured the soup into a plastic bowl. Plastics had outlasted china. He had only one china plate left, but the plastic things, though they had faded and roughened, were still going strong. Speaking of Lisa made him remember how she had hated using plastic. Not for the first time he caught himself thinking of her death as a release for both of them. He glanced guiltily at Muriel, as if she might be able to read his thoughts, but she still sat impassively, sipping her tea. He sat opposite and began to spoon up his soup. If there was going to be trouble, he thought, someone would have to take command here. So far they had managed without a leader, deciding everything between them. There had been so few choices that problems and disagreements had scarcely arisen. Now this could change. They had left the door open and could hear the sounds from outside quite clearly. There was some sort of disturbance out there. They could hear voices raised excitedly and the sound of bare feet splashing along the muddy path. Muriel put her mug on the floor and began to struggle out of her chair. Lucas took her hands and pulled her up and, for a moment, they both teetered off balance in the centre of the room. When they recovered, they saw the young man with the stick standing in the doorway looking in at them. 'What is it, Roy?' Lucas said.

'Smoke in the trees,' he answered. 'Come and see.' He turned away from them and started back. Lucas and Muriel followed more slowly, trying to avoid the worst of the mud.

It was true. Far away in the direction of the motorway a thin grey strand was drifting up from the trees. It hung in the air over a patch of conifers, thinned to invisibility and was followed by more. It was so faint that many of the villagers could not see it. There were still a few old pairs of spectacles amongst them but they were not ideally suited to anyone nowadays. In fact, even now one or two pairs were circulating, people peering experimentally through them before shaking their heads and passing them on. There was one good pair of binoculars and these were being used by one of the lookouts, a man in his thirties, who was scanning the distant woods patiently. The others stood round him looking anxiously in the same direction. After a time he shrugged and handed the binoculars to the man standing nearest to him.

'Can't see anything,' he told the crowd. 'Too many trees. I think a few of us should go down very cautiously and see what's going on.' He looked towards some of the younger men and said, 'I'll go myself of course, but I need two or three more'. A small group formed around him and prepared to move off down the hillside. Lucas was perturbed to see that they were all carrying heavy sticks or knives. At the same time as this was going on, some of the younger people were moving back through the village, walking past the huts to an area behind them, where Muriel's rabbits were penned. They moved purposefully in ones and twos and as if they were meeting by some previous arrangement, although they had not appeared to consult each other.

Something very curious was going on in the village, which Lucas had been watching for some time. There was a small area behind the huts and beyond the rabbit pens where a large stone lay on the grass looking rather like an enormous neglected grave. From somewhere or nowhere a superstition had grown that this stone had healing properties. The younger people pressed their injured limbs to it or simply sat leaning back against it if they felt unwell. From this they had moved on till they were practically worshipping it. Little bunches of flowers, withered apples and mushrooms were laid beside it. It reminded Lucas of shrines he had seen on the continent long ago, where faded plastic flowers lay at the feet of gaudily painted plaster saints. He had never seen anyone leave the offerings at the stone, but new flowers often appeared there. Apart from the youngsters, only Muriel visited this place. She said the vibes were good and had tried to move her rabbit pens nearer. After work she always knelt by the stone for a few minutes with her head bent and her hands flattened on its rough upper surface. She looked as if she was praying but said she was gathering strength – 'Tuning in to the infinite', as she put it. She said that, in scientific terms, it was something like recharging a car's battery but quicker. She watched the group now as they disappeared beyond the huts, but made no move to follow. Whatever this new cult was, she had no part in it. Her relationship with the stone was something private. She looked at Lucas and said 'Well, I don't think I can do anything here', and walked off towards her own hut. He noticed for the first time that she had begun to waddle and it saddened him.

The other group now began to move off down the hillside, led by the man who had been using the binoculars. They went very quietly one behind the other and, as soon as they reached the edge of the scrub beyond the cattle they slipped in between the tangle of gorse, hawthorn and brambles and disappeared like animals going to earth. Soon there was nothing to be seen of them except the rustle of leaves here and there. They had left the binoculars with the watchers and Lucas now sat with the rest of them on the rim of the embankment and waited his turn to scan the valley.

As the sun rose higher they relaxed, leaning back in the grass, enjoying the warmth and the bird song. They were a wild, ragged-looking group with their tattered clothes, weathered skin and flowing beards and hair. Water had to be carried from a stream some distance away and cleanliness was not one of their first priorities. Out in the open it was not too bad, but in the shacks there was a constant smell of clothes that had been worn too long over unwashed bodies. It was surprising how soon one became used to these conditions and accepted them. In the winter the older villagers grumbled and thought wistfully if uncertainly of their old comfortable days of central heating, clean clothes, soft blankets and fresh sheets. In summer, except when the rain kept on, they had become quite content to be a bit dirty and sit in the sun. Lucas found the life simple and pleasant. He had always been a great reader and even in winter he was quite happy to crouch over the fire with a book and a home-made candle. He wondered uneasily what changes could be moving towards them through the trees. Some would see any change as an improvement, but he was already regretting the probable passing of his easy life. It would have been good, he thought to sink into a mainly idle old age and die before he became too infirm. He would far prefer this to having his life uncomfortably prolonged by sophisticated medicine.

Towards the end of the afternoon there was a definite movement among the trees beneath them and the dog stood up and began to bark again. The scrub rustled, small branches shook and a line of men came out of the shelter of the trees and into the open field. They paused there for a moment, looking up, and then started towards the watchers, walking slowly one behind the other. There were only eight of them but they had captured the party who had gone out earlier. The captives walked at the back and had their hands fastened behind them. One man followed them and he carried a gun. Lucas and his party had stood up. They kept very still, watching the others intently. The young people had joined them, drawn by the barking dog. They waited too, but they all held heavy sticks. A short distance from them the newcomers stopped. They were hot and tired and dirty, but they were clean-shaven, well dressed and adequately if not obtrusively armed. Their leader came a little closer and spread his hands out towards them, palms first.

'We don't want trouble,' he said. 'I'm sorry we had to tie your men up, but they wouldn't stop attacking us. Perhaps you could tell them to stop it now, so we čan let them go.' He spoke to Lucas, perhaps because he was the oldest and most patriarchal of his group. His English was good, but he had a faint accent, possibly French or German. Lucas looked at the guns and said, 'No-one will attack you. There would be no point.' He glanced at the bound men and round at the young-sters behind him and they nodded their agreement. The young men still kept their sticks in their hands, but there was no aggression in the way they carried them.

'Can we come up?' the leader said. 'We've brought extra supplies. Perhaps we can give you something?'

'Beads for the natives,' Lucas thought bitterly.

The bound men were released and the whole party came up through the gap and into the enclosure. For a time the two groups were silent studying each other. All the dogs in the village were barking now. 'I'm sorry we couldn't come before,' the leader said at last when he had looked searchingly at them all and beyond them at their shacks. 'We had to keep out of your country for forty years. There could still have been some contamination. Things will get better from now on.'

At first the villagers held back, but soon they were shaking hands with the newcomers and admiring their clothes and the mass of gadgets they carried around with them. The leader stood in the centre of an excited group, demonstrating his camera by photographing everyone in turn and then handing them the prints.

Lucas stayed back watching. The new men could have come from another civilization and he supposed this was almost what they had done. They were as smooth and finished as if they had come off an assembly line. Nothing that they wore or carried had been made by anything but some highly sophisticated machine in a factory probably operated by robots. After a while he turned and walked quietly away. Through a gap between the huts he could see one other person. Muriel was kneeling with her hands pressed to the stone and he wished he could find comfort as easily. She was very still as if she had become part of the stone, some primitive monumental angel in flowing robes. Behind her, her rabbits nibbled busily at the grass, and the dogs, reassured by the behaviour of the villagers, were lying down again.

Lucas went into his shack and, although the sun still shone strongly in across the threshold, he shut the door behind him.

local writers who became friends while attending a creative writing class three years ago.

Philip Smith was born in North Wales in 1928 and was educated at Rhyl Grammar School and, variously, at the Universities of Bangor, Basle, Cambridge and Sussex. He worked as an English teacher until 1978, and began writing at evening classes in the Hanover Community Centre, Brighton. He is a member of the Hanover Writers' Group, which won the South East Arts Literary Group Prize for 1983. Nowadays he works and trains in psychotherapy, and also does jobbing gardening and office cleaning.

Tom Strachan was born in Marseilles in 1954. His stories have been published in several magazines and one has recently been included in *Stand One*, an anthology published by Gollancz. He has taught creative writing at adult education colleges in Dover and Deal and is now concentrating on his writing full-time.

Fred Urquhart was born in Edinburgh in 1912 and is one of Scotland's leading writers. His home is now in an isolated part of the Ashdown Forest where he has lived for over twenty-five years. He has published four novels, including *Palace of Green Days*, but is best known for his short stories and novellas. Twelve collections of these have appeared, the most recent being *Proud Lady in a Cage* and *Seven Ghosts in Search*.

Douglas Verrall was born in London in 1939. He has taught English and Drama in London, Hertfordshire and the USA and now lives in Hastings with his wife and four children. He has had plays produced by the Questors Theatre and the National Youth Theatre, and poems published by South East Arts. His wide range of interests includes playing the piano, acting at Hastings' Stables Theatre, supporting Hastings United Football Club and researching his family history.

Clare West, born in 1949, studied modern languages at Bristol University. She has travelled widely in Europe, and lectured in English for five years at a Libyan University. She now lives in Brighton with her second husband and one daughter; and for the last five years has been teaching English to foreign students in Hove and in Exmouth, but this leaves her time for her own writing.

ACKNOWLEDGEMENTS

South East Arts is the Regional Arts Association for the counties of Kent, East Sussex and Surrey. For many years the Association has published an annual anthology of poetry, written by people living in the three counties, under the title 'Poetry South East'.

This collection of 'Twenty Stories' follows the same path and seeks to introduce the vitality and talent of the region's prose writers. South East Arts acknowledges the care and attention given by the collection's editor, Francis King, in selecting the stories and wishes to thank the publishers, Martin Secker and Warburg, for their help and co-operation in ensuring that these works will be enjoyed by many readers in, and beyond, the South East.

The Barbara Campion Memorial Prize
This prize was made available through the kindness of Miss G. E. Campion of California, USA and is named after the poet Barbara Campion who lived in the South East region and contributed to the first anthology in the 'Poetry South East' series. The prize offers an award of £75 to the author of the work which the editor considers to be the most original or outstanding story to be included in the collection.

South East Arts wishes to express its gratitude to Miss G. E. Campion who made the award possible. The Association also wishes to thank Mrs M. Belsey of Gravesend, Kent, who donated a further sum to ensure the success of the prize.

This year the editor of this collection has awarded the Barbara Campion Memorial Prize to Fred Urquhart for his story *Kinderspiel*.

Trust Mother Audry

Thomas Hinde

They went out with Mother Audry to cut down the old tree: Sister Agatha, Sister Teresa, Sister Paula and Sister Martha. Sister Martha was the youngest.

The tree was an elm which had got the disease – it was a mercy, Mother Audry said, because it had always stood in the wrong place, making the chapel dark and gloomy, when it should be full of light. Sister Martha knew that Mother Audry would never have cut it down if it was alive.

Since they depended on wood for heating, it was twice a mercy. Wood had become terribly expensive, Mother Audry said. It might have been a mistake to buy the wood stove. Oh no, Sister Martha wanted to cry out, though she loved Mother Audry's honesty. We must pray for help, Mother Audry said. And, lo and behold, a couple of weeks later she had found that the old elm tree had died. It was as if God, seeing their need – and knowing it was in the wrong place – had decided to kill two birds with one stone. It was a kind of miracle, though when Martha had suggested this, Mother Audry had told her not to be silly, child.

The rebuke had made Sister Martha a little faint with joyful humility.

Three times a mercy, in fact, because the tree leaned away from the chapel so there was no need to employ a firm of tree surgeons, whose absurd price, Mother Audry explained, would have exceeded the value of the firewood. So instead she had borrowed an electric chain saw from the farm – not worrying them by saying why she wanted it. Watching that saw which she carried now in her strong left hand, Sister

Martha's heart beat fast with admiration. Given the chance she knew she would die for Mother Audry, though the thought alarmed her since it was surely for God that she should be ready to die, and she didn't feel the same enthusiasm for that idea.

As they went, Sister Agatha paid out the cable for the saw. She carried the coil in her left hand and paid it out with her right, and kept getting it caught up in her habit. Once when she bent to disentangle it she managed to knock her rimless glasses off her nose. Sister Martha wanted to giggle.

Sister Teresa carried a big iron wedge. She was tall and thin, with a pale oval face. She carried the wedge in her long pale hands in front of her chest, like an offering. Beyond her wimple her lips moved. She was praying.

Sister Paula carried a hammer with a long handle. She was almost as young as Sister Martha, but had a fat red face with spots. As soon as some faded, more would erupt. She carried the hammer in one fat red hand, which the scrubbing water made redder in this cold weather. It was, of course, because of her red hands and spots that Mother Audry had given her this responsible job. It was wrong of Sister Martha to hope the hammer would not be needed, but there was something she could not bear about the smug way Sister Paula carried it in her horrible red hand, while she herself had nothing to carry.

She couldn't even pray, like Sister Teresa, she was far too excited. This big tree coming crashing down. Mother Audry, with the blue saw in one strong hand and over her other shoulder a coil of rope – the tree leaned in the right direction, it was true, but the rope was to make sure. Though how they would tie it to the tree, Sister Martha could not imagine. Even Mother Audry could hardly climb up and tie it, dressed as she was.

She shouldn't have doubted. Mother Audry had also brought a ball of string. As soon as they stopped on the squelchy lawn and put down their things, those of them who had any, she produced it from a fold in her habit. One end she tied to a piece of brick, then let each of them try to throw this over one of the tree's branches. When Sister Agatha threw, it turned out she was treading on the rest of the string and the brick came back and hit her on the shin. Sister Martha could see that behind her glasses she was crying with pain and rage.

Fancy an old woman like that crying over such a thing. Sister Martha thought of Sister Agatha as an old woman, though she'd been told she was only forty-three.

Sister Martha tried next, but the brick only made a silly loop in the air then bounced along the path in front of them. When Sister Paula tried, she didn't throw at all but pushed it with her red hand and stumpy arm. It went an even shorter way.

'Well done, Paula,' Mother Audry said.

Sister Teresa tried next, and the brick went high, but unfortunately the string wasn't tied to it. As she watched someone else retrieve it her lips moved faster.

Then Mother Audry tried. She didn't throw it but bowled it. High up it went, over a branch on a level with the chapel's gutter, then came sploshing down onto the grass. When Mother Audry bowled the brick, her arms and legs spread out, she looked for a moment as if she was being crucified. Not the way Our Lord was, Sister Martha thought, but like St Patrick – who asked to be done diagonally, the same as the cross on his flag, so that he'd be different. Or was that St Andrew?

'Oh Mother!' Sister Paula exclaimed, in false amazement, because *of course* Mother Audry would be the one to succeed. Well that wouldn't do Sister Paula any good. The one thing Mother Audry hated was hypocrisy. She was good at detecting it, too. Now, when she smiled at Sister Paula it was with pity that she could be so false.

Mother Audry took the string from the brick and tied it to the end of the rope, then used the string to pull the rope over the branch. Next she tied the end of the rope in a slip knot round its other dangling side and pulled so that the slip knot went up tight against the branch. How helpless she made the rest of them seem.

Just as she finished, the icy wind came round the end of the chapel, catching their habits and blowing Sister Paula's so high she showed one fat red knee. Now Sister Martha did laugh, though she managed to put her hand to her mouth and turn it into a cough. The wind hardly moved the old tree. It stood there without leaves, tall and still, almost as if it knew what was going to happen to it. When Sister Martha looked up to its highest branches against the grey sky she felt giddy. There was something so sullen about it that just for an instant she wondered whether it *was* dead.

As for its trunk, it was so thick it made the little blue saw look a toy. How could such a little thing destroy something so big. Sister Martha wondered if she would be able to join her hands round it. She would have liked to try, and to fail, just to make them all realise what Mother Audry was going to do. But already Mother Audry was fitting the saw's plug into Sister Agatha's socket. The saw gave a whirring shriek, and they all jumped. Sister Martha wondered whether Mother Audry had done that on purpose. Oh, if only she knew about saws and things, so when Mother Audry said, 'Can any of you explain . . .' she could say modestly, 'I think so, Mother,' and casually push the right button and feel Mother Audry watching her in a new admiring way. But of course there was no need. From another fold in her habit Mother Audry had produced an instruction leaflet – trust Mother Audry.

Mother Audry studied it for a long time. Past her arm, Sister Martha saw diagrams of bits of saw and pictures of trees caught in the act of falling. Presently Mother Audry returned the leaflet to her habit and rolled back her sleeves to the elbow. Sister Martha had never seen Mother Audry's arms before. They were strong and grey.

Suddenly Sister Martha knew what was going to be needed. To cut where the diagram showed, close to the ground, Mother Audry would have to kneel on the wet grass. Instantly she ran back down the side of the chapel, took a kneeling mat from the pile in the porch, came panting back and set it on the ground by the tree. For a terrible moment she wondered whether she had done wrong. Perhaps holy things from the chapel should never be used for other purposes, even when it was Christ's work they were doing. But strangely, Mother Audry neither blamed nor praised, but hardly seemed to notice.

'I shall cut here,' she said. She pointed to the base of the trunk, not where it was closest to the chapel wall, not sideways to the chapel, but in between.

'To allow a forty-five degree safety exit,' Mother Audry said. She pointed with her right arm down the chapel wall, then down the path where they were standing. She kept her right arm extended in this direction (like Christ turning out the money changers) for several seconds, before they understood and pushed each other quickly off the path.

Turning to the tree, she knelt, bent forward and set the saw's chain against the trunk. Again it whirred and shrieked. Sister Paula put her fingers to her ears to flatter Mother Audry by showing how much she was frightening her, but Mother Audry wasn't looking. She just held the shuddering, shrieking saw in her strong hands as its blade cut into the tree. Already the cut was as deep as the blade. If any of them noticed that the flying chips of wood looked fresh, they didn't mention it. After all, you couldn't expect a big tree like this to die all at once.

'Now I shall cut a notch on the other side,' Mother Audry said. To get there, instead of passing between the tree and the chapel, she stepped right across the path where it would fall. Sister Martha drew in her breath and bit the inside of her lower lip. A second later she was ducking forward to bring Mother Audry her kneeling mat.

'Keep back, child,' Mother Audry shouted at her.

Sister Martha stood still and shaking. Mother Audry was often stern, but never before had she seemed angry. Her anger was not impersonal, but for Sister Martha, and Sister Martha knew that it had been there a long time and only these anxious moments had let it escape. I was just trying to help, she wanted to say, but these words terrified her by their suggestion of criticism, and by the way she knew they would make her burst into tears. Instead she prayed, 'Please God make me more sensible.'

Mother Audry knelt on the path and began to saw at the underside of the tree. First she made a horizontal cut, then she made a cut angled down to meet it. Soon the piece in the middle began to joggle about as the saw still screamed. Then it fell out onto the path. It was like a big pale slice of cake. Well done, Sister Martha wanted to call.

Mother Audry returned to this side of the tree and to her first cut. It was so deep now that the saw was making quite a dull noise. Steam was coming out of the cut and there was a delicious smell of singeing wood. Mother Audry stopped the saw. Without turning, she said, 'I think someone is standing in the safety exit.'

It was true.

Soon the cut seemed to be more than half way through the tree.

'Agatha and Martha, take the rope as far away as it will go,' Mother Audry said, 'but don't pull till I tell you. Teresa, bring the wedge.'

Mother Audry set the wedge in the cut and gave it a kick with the underside of her shoe to fix it there. Again the wind came round the end of the chapel and this time surely it did move the tree. And down by the cut, it surely creaked.

'Now Paula, hit the wedge with your hammer.'

So it had all been arranged. Sister Paula was going to strike the blow which would bring down the tree.

From twenty yards away by the rhododendrons where she held the limp rope, Sister Martha watched Sister Paula striking the wedge. Her little stunted body swinging the long-handled hammer was like a dwarf's. Her blows on the wedge rang in the cold air, those which hit it and which weren't bosh shots on the trunk.

'I shall take a turn,' Mother Audry said.

At her first blow – a real blow – there was a much louder crack and the whole tree from trunk to topmost branches gave a quiver. Sister Martha was filled with an awful sorrow for it. It seemed wrong that they should be destroying something so big and old at so little cost to themselves.

'Right you are, Paula,' Mother Audry said, handing the hammer back to her. For the first time she gave a thin smile, as if even she was a little excited by what was going to happen, though more by Paula's excitement at the triumph she was about to have.

Sister Paula wound herself up for a bigger blow. She was bursting with pride, even from away by the rhododendrons Sister Martha could tell. She hit the wedge hard, but not cleanly. The head of the hammer must have been mostly beyond it because it whipped the handle out of her hand and the whole hammer spun away round the tree, finishing on the path at its far side.

But the blow had been enough. Now loud cracking and splitting sounds came one after another.

'Pull,' shouted Mother Audry.

Sister Agatha and Sister Martha pulled. At the same time Sister Martha looked up at the tree's upper branches, now swaying down towards them at terrifying speed. That was why she didn't see exactly what happened.

Afterwards it was all explained. Sister Paula, seeing the tree about to fall on the hammer which she had just used to knock it down, had made a dash to rescue it. Mother Audry had screamed at her and rushed after her, but tripped over Sister Agatha's cable and landed on her face. Perhaps the fall winded her because she had seemed to make no attempt to rise but had just lain there while the enormous tree gathered speed and came crashing down. Its trunk fell across her back.

'She's dead,' screamed Sister Teresa.

'Of course she's dead,' screamed sister Agatha and was sick down the front of her habit.

'Oh oh oh,' screamed Sister Paula. 'It was me, it was me,' she screamed. 'Oh, oh, oh.'

Sister Martha ran to her where she stood staring down at the parts of Mother Audry they could see. Where her body emerged from below the great grey trunk horrible soft bulges seemed to fill her black habit.

'Come quickly,' Sister Martha said. She still couldn't touch Sister Paula. Then she did. She took Sister Paula's little red hand and made her run with her for help.

'It wasn't you,' she shouted as they ran. 'It wasn't anyone's fault.' But secretly she knew this wasn't true. It was she herself who had done it. God had known about her jealousy for Sister Paula and had said, 'All right, I'll show you where such wicked thoughts lead.'

in,' she continued, not really expecting to be heard, 'but he was too rough and Barbara got upset and Johnso objected, but we're alright now, aren't we, Johnso?'

He had never really wanted the son to be called John after him and 'Johnso' he hated, but never let it be known.

He could have tried to explain but other things would have been said, perhaps in front of the children, and there was no time for unpleasantness. 'Life is too short for unpleasantness' was another of the grand, philosophical statements he declared to his growing family from time to time.

He climbed slowly and deliberately up the stairs back to his marriage and thought about the day that had been. An odd sort of day without the phone call. He had observed that his Head of Department had been away for the first time in seven years and he felt he ought to have behaved like a mouse while the cat was away but, lacking the effort and initiative, he hadn't, and smiled wryly to himself that he hadn't. One of the staff had celebrated his fortieth birthday that day and he had joked about being forty once too (in fact he was nearer fifty) and the joke had fallen flat. He had collected the Family Allowance as usual (it was a Tuesday and Tuesdays seemed to come round with a more alarming frequency than the other days of the week) and the local Post Office was manned by two different ladies, one of them an attractive Indian. Were the usual ladies on holiday? An odd time of the year for a holiday. Had they retired or died mysteriously? What had happened? He had asked too many questions already in the classroom that day and had now been too tired to ask about the absent women for fear of being transported into some new dimension.

'It wasn't your mother, then?'

'No.'

The lie was reinforced. Easier the second time.

He sat down. This evening he would retreat into fiction. It was the only way to survive. Which half-started novel would he try to finish reading? Was there a good movie on television? Retreat from reality was vital. Thinking-about-the-dying-millions therapy wouldn't work this time. It had to be fiction of some sort: light, easy fiction. But there was nothing he felt he could turn his attention to. He sat there stunned, 'dreaming' his mother would have called it, while the newscaster pronounced the latest catastrophes, the sparrow chirped weakly

and the boy and girl thought up their next differences of opinion. He wanted – banal thought – to hide behind a stone, to be alone with some ultimate, divine Comforter.

'We'll borrow a cage,' the wife said.

No reply.

'A cage. For the sparrow.'

'A cage. Good idea, darling.'

There is no ecstasy, he quoted in his thoughts, as the telephone rang again and his wife went down to answer.

Dingo

F. Bennett

From all the dogs roaming the world, unwanted, unloved, I had to give my affection to a half-bred dingo, the wild dog of the Australian outback. This bitch that became mine, gradually digging her way into my heart with her natural skill and loving ways, was no beauty, except in my eyes. She was lop-eared, long-legged, her fur hard, yellow from her dingo and kelpie forebears, this last breed being the sheep dog reared on so many sheep stations for their working strain. Her golden eyes were her one redeeming feature; their shining depth showed a fine intelligence. As a pup she displayed no sign of the killer instinct of the dingo, the reason they are hated, hunted, trapped and poisoned on the big cattle and sheep stations. One dingo will, in a night, wound many sheep in its desperate chase through a herd, seeking a victim; or a pack of those wild dogs will hunt down a cow with a new-born calf, separate them from a mob of cattle, and worry the weakened cow until they can part her from her offspring, when they rush in for the kill. Call a man a dingo down under and he'll feel wounded for life; it's considered the most deadly insult.

Boundary riding in the Georgina country, bordering the Northern Territory, the far north-west cattle country of Australia, I came upon this pup. Mine was a lonely job but a good one, that is if you find enjoyment in the wide open spaces of outback Aussie, which I did. I got to know and love every tree: the Coolibar, Gum, Box, even the vast, dry, empty paddocks and acres of Spinnifex; tufts of thorny growth that seem to exist without water, for it was drought country, often missed by the yearly monsoonal rains. Flowers would not

146

survive the scorching heat of those vast plains, but flocks of birds, budgerigars, green in undulating flight, huge white cockatoos, vivid parrots, gave colour and life as they flew around or rested like gorgeous blooms on the trees.

Happily I rode the paddocks, repairing broken fences; reporting to the station manager movement of cattle; herding small mobs back to the paddock from whence they had strayed. They say a cow or bull will go through any fence, if it has a mind to do so, and I have often seen them skilfully easing their way through the fencing, built as it is outback with stout posts run through with several rows of wiring.

I carried my tucker in the saddle bag, bread, meat, tea, and at noon, after a hard morning's riding, boiled my quart pot over a bushman's fire, a few dry leaves and twigs, soon ignited, enjoying a brief respite from the blazing heat around me.

My home was a hut, not too badly furnished with all the necessities for living, situated ten miles from the station homestead, from whence I rode out six days a week, happy in the freedom of my life, the continual blue skies, the peacefulness of it all.

I'd settled down to enjoy my break, a quick meal and brief shuteye, when I spotted this pup. There was movement amongst some nearby lignum bushes, and a small bundle of fur, all yellow, golden eyes, came waggling through the bush. Apart from birds and cattle, animal life in that vast countryside was rare; a stray 'roo, a rabbit or so was all you would expect to see, and in the heat of high noon nothing ever stirs in the stillness and silence of outback Australia. I called her to me and after a while she came and let me stroke her. I fed her cooled tea, diluted from a nearby billabong, which seemed to go down a treat. She might have been abandoned by Abos gone walkabout; there were signs of a deserted camp, bag humpy and bower shed, old bones and the leavings of a big camp fire. 'You're lucky,' I told her, 'you wouldn't have survived long in this heat.'

So Lucky she became. I propped her upon the pommel of my saddle, steadied my bay gelding while I mounted, and rode for home. It was Saturday, the heat was past bearing.

I became the devoted slave of my Lucky; I lavished upon her round yellow body all the love of a lonely man, and watched her grow from a hard ball of fur to a lean young bitch. I loved

the look of her: golden eyes, slim muscular body, white-tipped tail, held erect like a pennant in movement.

Early morning, when I rode out on the night horse to round up my small string of working horses, yarding them to select my mount for the day, she would run beside me, leaping high, somersaulting with the sheer joy of living; and when it was necessary to check a straying animal she was there, young as she was, heeling them, wheeling them; she was all a cattle dog should be, which was strange considering her lineage, but that's the way it turns out sometimes.

She was always by my side when I rode out on my inspection of the fences, and when she became tired, being not yet fully grown, I would mount her on the pommel, and we rode together in close, happy companionship. My horse made no objection; a boundary rider's horses are dependable animals, quiet, steady, sometimes half-draft; a frisky mount, liable to pull away, is the last thing you need, riding the outback fences.

I fed her the best, plenty of raw meat and big bones. Daily, with small tweezers, I removed from her body, the corners of those golden eyes, deep inside her ears, the ghastly ticks that plague station dogs; little spider-like creatures fat with blood, that cling to and feed on certain animals. It was a nauseating job, grabbing them and pulling them free, killing them, but I was dead sure my Lucky would not be plagued by them. She repaid me with her devotion; my shadow by day, sleeping beside me at night. Hurt beyond measure if I ever reprimanded her, her golden eyes would regard me with unbelieving sorrow as she cringed to the ground, bewildered and tortured by the absence of my usual affection.

She was only ten months old when the boss drove out early one morning to my hut. This was unusual, he always contacted me by the station phone every evening after I'd returned from my daily round of inspecting and repairing. Perhaps the lines were down; there'd been a quick, scurrying storm the previous evening, fierce winds, thunder to rock you backwards, early monsoonal rain, heavy, hurtling straight down from the heavens. Lucky had been a little scared and sheltered under the kitchen table; now she growled at this intruder as he stood framed in the doorway.

The boss eyed my pet with distaste as we chatted for a few minutes about the work in hand and then 'get those cleanskins

in Adelaide paddock,' he instructed me, 'and drown that flaming dingo.' Aussies are like that, especially in the great outback; downright, forthright. Station life is hard, serious, there's no time for mucking about. If the boss gives an order it is carried out at once.

I should have known my dingo pup would never be tolerated on that cattle station; I had known and had ignored the inevitable issue; now I had to face and come to grips with the result of my foolishness.

As I saddled up and prepared for my ride, hurt and irresolute, I found my eyes continually straying to my beloved Lucky as she sat before me, erect, eyes on mine. With the infallible sixth sense that animals of all species possess, she knew, she was waiting for my verdict.

Of course I couldn't do it; I could no more hurt her, drown her, shoot her, than jump off Sydney Bridge; my whole recent life had been geared to her care and protection. She was everything to me and a great help too in my daily work. The boss, I told myself, was being very unreasonable. I climbed slowly into the saddle and rode for Adelaide paddock. Lucky ran beside me, leaping, somersaulting, coming to heel when I whistled.

The cleanskins grazed happily in Adelaide paddock; I approached them cautiously, Lucky at heel; one false move and they'd be gone with the wind. It had been a long hard ride, an early start and now, at full noon, the sun blazed, scorching down. After the big muster, these were the ones missed, unbranded; they had to be rounded up, brought into the stockyard for branding.

I was excited, elated; in that vast country you were not always lucky enough to ride upon them. I cantered towards them, cows, calves, young steers; they bellowed at my approach, left their grazing and moved onwards.

I had them on the go, cantering I moved them homewards. I looked for Lucky, couldn't see her; she was still a pup, it had been a long hard grind, I was expecting too much from her. My work must come first; it was exhilarating, rewarding to be herding home those cleanskins.

But continually my eyes searched the far paddocks as I wheeled and herded the stragglers; I looked for movement, any sign of my pup. Now that the herd was on the go I'd have galloped to her, let her ride on the pommel as so often before.

The paddock was starkly bare, just browned acres of grass-land, no bush or tree to hide her from me. My Lucky never returned. When I'd yarded the cleanskins, I rode out to find her, searching the paddocks, longing for a sight of her. I searched until the sudden southern night wiped away all light; she was not to be found; she was half dingo; I could only hope that her natural savage inheritance of self-preservation would protect her. I felt weakened by my physical effort and drained of all life's meaning. Sadly I rode the trail to my lonely hut.

Life went on; station work is demanding, the constant care of animals, fences, equipment. My days were busy; it was the long nights when I felt so lost, lonely, hurt by the absence of my beloved pup. I missed her so much it was torture sitting there, trying to read by my carbide light. I'd find jobs, mend things, but the hours to bedtime were still so long, so empty. Station dogs are always housed in the home paddock adjacent to the night horse or the big garages; their life is severe, forever chained, small kennels, meagre food; they are bred to work, this being the only time they are unleashed and allowed to run. My Lucky had broken all rules, enjoying the home comforts of my hut, sharing my life; she'd been my constant shadow; I missed her at every turn.

I was trailing the station milkers, a small mob of Jerseys and Friesians. For reasons of their own they'd gone through the home paddock fences and I'd been sent to find them.

They'd gone through all fences, I found, heading for that vast wilderness of far west Australia. I tracked them, not easy in that drought country, and after a hard ride had come upon them, still heading westwards.

Being domestic animals they were easy to handle and at sight of me they turned and headed for home. I was fond of them, big lumbering cows, gentle as babies; I knew them all by name and was urging them onwards when I became aware of the yellow shadows skulking behind the stragglers; a pack of dingos who looked lean and hungry enough to attack; there would be little food for them in that bare country.

At a distance they circled now; this was something I'd never experienced before, although I knew the savagery of those wild dogs when hungry. They were circling the herd and me, awaiting the right moment for attack, the cows leaping, bucking and bellowing in fear.

And then I saw my Lucky, leaner, full grown, she ran with the mob, snarling! So she'd gone to the pack! I'd thought so, guessed this must be the reason for her disappearance; I'd known that if she'd wanted to, she'd have found her way back to me.

I whistled fiercely, the old whistle she'd known so well, piercing, commanding her to come to me. I fell from my saddle, embracing her as she leapt into my arms, licking my face, jumping high, somersaulting to show her joy at our meeting.

I fondled her, whispering words of endearment; tears came to my eyes as I felt the warmth of her yellow fur and saw once again the golden gleam of her beautiful eyes. Now I'd never let her go.

The dogs had fallen back a bit, still circling. I clutched my long-lost pet to me, hugging her; Lucky moved restlessly, licking my face. I began to form vague plans in my mind, how to hold her, keep her from the pack. It was my responsibility to protect the milkers, to get them safely home, and yet I believe, in that great moment of joy and relief at finding my pet again, I would have abandoned the cows for the love of that bitch.

A big Jersey bellowed high in fear, kicking at the yellow shape that snapped at her heels.

Then the hard ground was echoing with the drumming of hooves; a mob of riders hurtled towards me, galloping hard, scattering dust tree high. They were my mates from the station, I could recognize them as they drew nearer; they were the stockmen and ringers with whom I rode at the annual muster; now, seeing the danger, they were riding to help me.

Alerted and scared by the thundering mob of horses, the dingos scattered in alarm, then, swerving into a tight pack, moving as one animal, following their leader, were off, racing away in a frightened bunch.

The horsemen galloped to my side; I looked for Lucky, whistled frantically as I saw her streaking to join the pack, her long slim body flat out, tail held high like a waving pennant. Soon she was up with the leader, heading for the never-never land of far west Australia.

Out of the Forest

Jack L. Phillips

In the beginning there was Night, and the hand of Night was heavy and monstrous and lay across the Earth so that the Earth slept.

Then was Night beaten back by Day, and the forest, which was everywhere, opened its eyes and was struck blind by the Sun. So did the forest, once stalwart, become weak and confused and was divided of itself and again divided so that each part became separated from the others and lived on in ignorance of them.

And it came to be that in one part of the dark, living forest there stood a house.

(Principia: 1–3)

'Clumsy child!' She stood over him, stiffly bent, bony anger thrusting at his face. 'You stupid, clumsy child!'

The words, hurled through the pale air, shattered like angry glass against the stone and the slivers armed themselves against the house, invading it, rattling along the passages, glancing from the chipped pillars and abutments, dissipating among the cracked and ratty ledges, seeping beneath a hundred locked and never-opened doors. The echoes drowned, the house resumed its soft decay.

The boy stood uneasily upon the flags, sleeve scuffing at his nose. 'It was an accident,' he said.

She regarded him sternly. 'You must beg forgiveness nonetheless.'

He stood looking up at her, at his back the unkempt fountain, green-spouted, dry, its huge bowl littered: crumpled paper, glass, dried-up pellets of dung, and beside the marble rim the ikon, shattered.

'But it was an accident,' he insisted, 'I dropped it, I didn't mean to break it.'

The woman stretched out her hand towards him, her voice gone softer now: 'Come, we'll pray together.'

He regarded her silently for a moment, then knelt, weeping, and with wretched fingers tried to make amends. Fitting the brittle splinters one into the other, the holy-ridden face mocking him with awful solemnity and down one saintly cheek a cicatrice of broken wood stained darkly wet with tears. Clutched in his anxious hands the fitted pieces cramped, almost mended, then buckled, flipped, and fell. The clattered wood, hallowed edges dulled beyond repair: meek mouth, beard and broken halo, the flaking vestige of an eye to ridicule his clumsiness.

Anger quickened in his throat and in a sudden weakly fury the boy lifted his foot and smashed the booted heel down into the painted fragments of the face.

The woman stiffened as if stabbed, staring at the splinters on the floor. The boy, fearful now, watched her, wondering what form her retribution would take.

Slowly she raised her gaze and looked at him: the small pale face, nervous mouth, and behind the dark clever eyes the edge of triumph. No remorse, no guilt. He's like a young animal, she thought, testing his strength. She turned from him, catching his relief as she dropped her gaze, and began slowly to climb the stairs.

'Where are you going?'

She stopped, her black back stiff, white fingers resting on the balustrade. 'To pray for you,' she answered, hoping, hoping he would offer to accompany her.

He stood looking up at her, the climbing footsteps faltered and went on, a silence, then nothing save the myriad unheard movements of the house: plaster crumbling damply on a floor, dark scuttles puffing dust into demented webs, the sibilance of softly-uttered prayer.

Of all sins that of Sacrilege shall be deemed unforgiveable and whomsoever doth become guilty of It then shall he become as a scattering of dust and vengeance upon him will be as a dark eternal wind, driving him hither and thither and he shall know no rest.

(Principia: 43)

The boy was in bed. They had eaten their supper in silence: he had made it plain he was not ready for a reconciliation. A first victory is not easily relinquished and throughout the meal he had kept up a forced self-assurity that effectively blocked all conversation. He did, however, accompany her to the little chapel, kneeling beside her at the prie-dieu as he had done every evening since he left the crib. Eyes closed, fingers childishly steepled as he quickly whispered. 'Blessed be the Father, blessed be the Son . . .' Ritual is not so easily displaced, she thought.

Then later, alone in the deep chair, as outside the trees moaned and rustled in the darkness. She was getting old: she had seen it reflected in his glance this morning and again this evening as they ate. He was growing up quicker than she had realized. Or had been willing to acknowledge. These years! Past now, so long, so swift. Study and prayer. The great painted books, catechisms, raw knees and cold clasp of prayer at dawn, she teaching, him learning, verse upon verse, chapter upon chapter, lamplight, the comfort and extravagance of incense, the rising of her hopes. And then this morning! It seemed that after all, she had failed to teach him anything. Only fear! Yet fear alone might save him.

Then be it known that when He doth come, as He most surely will, it will be in the guise most fitting for His purpose. And He shall dwell among the people and they shall call Him 'Lord' and their goodness shall be drained from them and their souls taken into bondage.

(Praemonitus: I, 23–24)

They walked along the narrow path: the woman and the boy. On either side the sunlight fell through the great leaping greenness of the forest, landing in wide patches upon the tops of the bracken, turning the soft shadows into dark caves.

She stepped carefully, pinching her hem clear of the undergrowth with matronly precision. The child explored the path ahead, calling, stooping, flickering like a bright flag among the trees. Sometimes, in spite of her care, she became entangled and he would rush back gallantly to her assistance.

Whenever he found something of special interest he waited impatiently for her to catch up, eager to point out the high precarious ball of a squirrel's drey, the pastel fragments of a

plundered egg, or a huge old oak, cloven by some summer storm, dying slowly, splendidly, and she, pointing at a long black beetle feeding on the wound, whispered: 'Beware! The Devil's coach-horse!' With such mock ferocity that they both jumped backwards, landing in a heap, giggling at their own foolishness.

Towards midday they rested. Together they laid the food out upon a clean white cloth. The forest absorbed their presence as they ate, relaxing its vigilance into a drowsing quiet punctuated by long dipping bird-calls, the drone of insects, leafy rustlings. Life went on. The woman dozed.

When she awoke he was sitting in front of her holding a posy of wild flowers. He held them loosely so as not to bruise their stems. Bidding her to sit forward, he knelt behind her and twined them in her hair and, when he had finished, he looked at her and said: 'There, now you are Queen of the woods and all the creatures must obey you.'

She laughed, stood up and made a curtsey to him. 'If I am Queen then you must be my prince!'

'Oh no, I'm the Wizard of the Forest, weaver of spells and evil!'

He grimaced and crouched, did a mincing little dance and recited, rhyming the words in a childish couplet: 'I live in a hollow tree, with a toad and a bat for companeee!' He stretched the last syllable out and down into a long, witching cry. From a thicket nearby, a blackbird yattered and fled in anxious swoops.

Unamused, she turned away and commenced to gather up the remnants of the meal. When she spoke again her voice was flat, weary, as if the sunshine in which she had rested had drained her of all hope. 'Come,' she said, 'we still have a little way to go.'

They started off again along the narrow path, the woman moving now with a sense of urgency, her walk less graceful, her robe dipping unattended in the debris of the forest, catching up, snagging, tearing a little here and there. Behind her the boy concentrated only on the path beneath his feet and on the flowers that fell limply, unnoticed, from her hair.

Thus they moved, the woman and the boy, apart from the forest and at odds with it, the great trees languishing and

charged with heat, the insects rising in sudden fretful clouds, and the forest commencing to inflict on them its thousand twiggy wounds.

Recklessly now, the woman stabbed her way through the woods. The path died out but still she pushed and fought her way ahead, hair plucked wild, robe crazed, and the boy struggling fearfully behind, welted, lashed, his face grimed with tears.

Suddenly they burst into a clearing. A glade with flowers perched in blue squadrons beneath the trees and from a heavy bough a cage, man-shaped, flaked with rust, and inside the bones of something long, long, locked away.

Then the people seized Him and brought Him before her, saying: 'Behold, here is thy Lord, thy Prince of Darkness'. And she saw that her people were angered and afraid and so commanded that He be taken to a certain place and bound in iron and therein left to perish.

(Resurgam: I, 73.)

She stood behind him, her hands gripping his shoulders. Before them hung the cage: wide, coopered bands heavy with rivets, the chain rust-wrapped and knotted almost carelessly around the bough. They had been swift, she thought, quick and hard and clever. Hands so used to pulling, gripping, tying. As if their life's-work had been just a preparation for those moments.

Beneath her fingers she felt the flat young muscles bunch as he twisted to look up at her. Fiercely she shifted her grip and clenching his chin between her thumb and fingers, forced his head back and up.

'Look there!' she hissed. 'Look hard and long on what happened here!'

Wincing beneath the pressure of her fingers, the boy looked up at the figure resting inside the cage, the picked bones outstretched to form a cross and on the forehead, on the skull, high above the caverns of the face, a V seared blackly in the bone.

Whimpering, he screwed his eyes shut and tried once more to turn away. She gripped him tighter.

'No! Please! Let me go!' His scream pierced the stillness of the surrounding forest and, this time, she relaxed her hold.

Sobbing, he turned to bury his face in her body. She clasped him then, kneeling, rocking gently to his sobs.

How he screamed, she thought, the woods had echoed to his screams. The torches smoking greasily, those gleeful brutish faces at the fire and the iron glowing as he screamed,

The boy was staring into her face, awaiting an explanation. He watched her lips move but she made no sound, only hugged him closer, pressed him closer against her as they knelt together in the returned stillness of the glade. The sun on their bare heads, her bowed head, the forest around them, hushed and neutral and the cage upon its bough like some huge malignant fruit.

She remembered feeling flattered. At first flattered, then numb, yes, numb with joy. Her feet and fingertips had tingled with pleasure. Abruptly she released the child, rose swiftly to her feet and moved away, her back towards him, one hand plucking at the bosom of her robe. Her voice, when at last she spoke, was barely above a whisper: 'It was something within him, something he couldn't overcome.' Her words, shame, falling like dark feathers and the boy, spellbound, on the grass.

She had asked him why. They had been alone, she heavy with child, blooming, and death had crept into the room. Why? 'I love you – never doubt it,' he had said.

She turned to face the child. He stood up. His face was taut, the skin stretched tight across his cheekbones. She reached out her hand but he ignored it, walking past her, leading the way back into the forest.

Together they left the clearing. She looked back once, at the stillness of the glade and their footprints in the grass and among the flowers from which rose the sharp, crushed scent of wild garlic.

The Vocation

Beryl Lewin

V era's was the hand that waved, invisible, never catching the attention of the teacher. She was the odd one left when teams were picked, the girl they all forgot when numbers were checked on school journeys.

Later, she was the plain girl who went to dances with a pretty friend, was placed by hostesses at the end of dinner-tables or next a vacant chair. Ignored by waiters, taxis, shop assistants, bus drivers, often unrecognized by old acquaintances: as she grew older she began in desperation to invent small quirks of character for herself, so that the people she met should have something by which to distinguish her. Searching her mind and noticing a spider scuttling across her bathroom floor, she became on the instant a confirmed arachnephobe. To be truthful she had never liked the creatures and now she could shudder convincingly and swear that they made her feel positively ill. Soon afterwards, a mild distaste for shell-fish became a full-fledged allergy, so that at wedding receptions she could recoil at the prawn cocktail and enjoy the agreeable flurry that would ensue while the substitute grapefruit was brought to her. At least she would now be remembered after parties for her food allergy, even if both hosts and guests forgot her name.

Gradually, in this way, she assembled a package of passions and prejudices which almost, she felt, amounted to a complete personality. People could say of her 'Oh, that's the girl who reads Wells and Walpole', 'She's mad on Humphrey Bogart', 'She always uses "French Fern"', 'Wears nothing but shades of blue'. She was not naturally very musical, but at the time she

had decided to build her personality into something recognis-
able by other people (even if not to herself) she was lent some
Britten records by an acquaintance (she had nothing as positive
as a friend). Instantly she realised that here was a composer
with an individuality sufficiently marked to be recognised
even by such a musical illiterate as herself. Others she might
confuse, but she would always know those clear sweet notes of
Peter Pears rising delicately from their pianoforte settings,
weaving through horns and strings, so she cultivated this
taste, playing the records again and again until she could never
be mistaken.

So she continued her life, such as it was; home and office,
divided by suburban trains and south coast holidays, and over
the years assembled a neat collection of carefully cultivated
traits, all ready to be opened for others to view, like the
contents of a china display cabinet or a butterfly collection. As
she became older, she thought she detected a growing indifference to her foibles among the people she knew. Their eyes
glazed and averted when she enlarged on her terror of heights,
detestation of Liberace, love of Spain and interest in bull-
fighting. They had heard it all before and were bored – almost
as bored as she was herself. Once again she was registering as a
non-person. She began to dress in very brilliant colours,
played her radio loudly, wrote letters to the papers, entered
competitions. But with almost everyone else wearing increasingly garish clothes, her own purple kaftans or yellow
culottes passed unobserved. The neighbours, their ears covered with Sony Walkmans or deafened by constant exposure
to discos, ignored her blaring wireless. Her letters were never
published, she won no contests and her attempts to join radio
phone-in programmes were always frustrated – either all lines
were engaged, or she was invited to 'hold on please', so that,
although sometimes her name was taken, her opinions were
never sought and her views (such as they were) never
expressed upon the air. She wrote to 'Any Answers' and
'Woman's Hour', volunteered her services for 'You, the Jury'
and 'Question Time', sent in record requests; all without avail.
She began to doubt her own existence.

Eventually the day came when she was made redundant,
although she felt this was only a statement of something that
had been a fact for many years. On her last day at the office

there was the presentation of a travelling-clock. She could imagine that most of the people who subscribed to this had said 'Who?' as the usual card was circulated for signature with donations. All had no doubt contributed the minimum decency allowed for this parting gift.

Her parents had died some years before, at which time she had moved into a flat, forming part of a converted Victorian house, more convenient for travelling to the office. Hence she had lost touch with childhood neighbours and had so far made little contact with the somewhat transient population of the decaying Clapham street. Without her colleagues now, she began more than ever to feel herself to be invisible. Day after day, unheard, unseen, or so it seemed, she glided among the indifferent shoppers, ignored, even unjostled, until she felt ready to climb on a bench in the shopping precinct, to scream and wave her arms or hold up a placard 'saying 'I'm here. Notice me!' But what would be the point? she thought, wearily. They would hurry by, obsessed with their own affairs, barely raising their eyes from their shopping lists; perhaps saying 'It's her time of life' or telling their children 'Take no notice. She's just a bit dotty.'

She took to going regularly to the park with stale bread and bacon rinds to feed the birds by the ornamental lake. At least they did not ignore her, but crossed the water to her with a fluttering rush. She would spin out her little time of glorious attention to the uttermost; throwing the titbits in different directions, so that the coots and mallards were obliged to paddle frantically first one way, then another, and the strutting pink-toed pigeons to hustle greedily from side to side as her whim dictated. But inevitably the bag would empty, the faithless feathered mendicants would turn their attention elsewhere and she would walk back, hands and heart as empty as the bag, across the deck-chaired grass.

Her greatest delight then was to be recognized and even, joy of joys, actually spoken to by someone, anyone; the meter-reader, insurance agent, or milkman rattling by on his float. Sometimes she encountered these people out of context in their Sunday clothes and could not herself immediately re-member who they were. Thus the baker (against whom she waged a weekly war because of the staleness of his bread) she met once in the park with wife and children; unoveralled,

uxorious, smug over a picnic tea, romping with a yellow frisby. He greeted her effusively, perhaps from shame at the evident freshness of the sandwiches on the plastic cloth in comparison with anything he had supplied to her, though she doubted his propensity to embarrassment from such a cause. But, rascally though she knew him to be and doubtless indifferent to her very existence, his words sent a glow through her and she looked about to see if other strollers in the park had noticed the encounter. Here was she, a person in her own right, being recognised and addressed by another person!

From then on she went regularly to the park at that particular time on Sundays and was able to repeat the meeting several times. There was a local greengrocer, too, whom she saw jogging in the early mornings and who would sometimes hail her as she took in her milk, thus giving her a sense of her own reality even before breakfast. But best of all were the chance meetings in crowded places, often with people she hardly knew; perhaps a plumber who had replaced a defective ball-valve, or the bank-clerk who had cashed her cheque the previous day. She would confront them squarely and if they looked a little vague at first, she would swiftly give them a clue to her identity by thanking them enthusiastically for whatever small service they had rendered her and would soon be enjoying an animated conversation with them, often no doubt to their considerable astonishment. All the while part of her attention would be elsewhere; resting on the unheeding passers-by, saying to them 'Look! I am a person, known to this other person. He remembers me, he knows where I live and what I do. Do you not wish that you, also, could know me and be included in my circle? Are you not fascinated to hear how this conversation may end or to guess what may have been said before?'

She sought and assiduously cultivated these trivial encounters with neighbours and tradespeople. However there were still whole days when no single incident occurred to verify her existence and she then began to consider some more drastic method of drawing attention to herself. She had been to the doctor with a number of minor complaints, but he only prescribed tranquillizers or antibiotics and advised her to take a holiday. But waiting at the surgery, she was infected with the germ of an idea, the contagion coming from the

occasional appearance of slings and crutches. She must have an accident!

This surely ought not to be too difficult to achieve; after all, car-drivers had never seen her when she had tried hitch-hiking as a young girl, so there was no reason to suppose that, now in middle-age, she would be any more visible to them stepping unexpectedly off the kerb. Obviously there would be a certain amount of pain involved, but the more she considered the idea, the more positive she became that it would be worth it. The medical attention, the hospital visits, the conspicuousness of her injuries (for she had made up her mind that they *would* be conspicuous); all would combine to make her irresistibly noticeable. Passers-by, complete strangers, would react with pity or curiosity. They might even flinch with horror, if she were to be badly scarred. Even that would be preferable to their present total indifference. She began seriously to consider the possibility of a wheel-chair. After all, if she were to be crippled, that would mean constant attendance, endless concern by others for her welfare, special arrangements to be made wherever she went. Yes, on the whole, she thought such an effect would more than compensate for any pain and inconvenience.

The difficulty was, of course, that she could not absolutely guarantee even partial disability, and this at first seemed to present an almost insuperable problem. Then she remembered a thriller she had read, which involved a bewitching young girl, wholly confined to a wheel-chair, following a car-crash in which her parents had been killed. On being confronted by a house-breaker, the girl had risen from her chair and taken several steps across the room. It transpired that her illness had been psychosomatic, induced by the shock of the accident. Very well then, she herself would have psychosomatic paralysis and, even if doctors could prove that her nervous system was intact, she was sure they could not prove that she did not have such an illness if she simply refused to move.

This, then, was her plan and she determined to put it into effect at the earliest possible opportunity. Accordingly, one wet Friday afternoon, when the pavements were crowded with busy people obsessed with weekend shopping and the roads congested with home-going cars and loaded lorries making for the coast, she put on an inconspicuous rain coat,

for once seeking to be unobserved, and set off for the town centre. She had given considerable thought to the location of her so-called accident, bearing in mind the maxim that 'time spent in reconnaissance is never wasted', and had eventually selected a blind bend near a railway arch where the noise of frequent trains tended to mask the sound of on-coming vehicles. Choosing her moment with care, she hesitated at the kerb until she gauged that the rapidly approaching Cortina was too close to stop and then stepped confidently forward, bracing herself for the impact. The most terrifying thirty seconds of her life followed for, as the vehicle braked and a man shouted, she turned her head away and to her sick horror saw an enormous container-lorry bearing down on her from the other direction. Her entrails congealed, her legs turned to rubber as she realized in that moment that this monster could crush her to extinction or maim her beyond anything she had intended. This was not part of her plan at all, not at all.

She wavered, stumbled forward, recovered herself and then, suddenly, the crisis was over and she found herself on the far pavement somehow, intact and feeling rather foolish. There was a confused jabber of sound behind her. Already a small crowd had collected, but for once she did not wish to be the centre of attention and walked quickly, if shakily, away without looking back. She must have been mad, she thought, to imagine that she would get off with a *restricted* accident. It was the essence of an accident that it should be unpredictable. She might easily have been killed; as it was she had got away unhurt and neither of these alternatives had been planned. She hurried towards the familiar turning to her road, rounded the corner and nearly collided with the woman from next door. Swerving, she apologised, then noticed that the woman was leading a small dog, evidently a new acquisition.

'How sweet! A Jack Russell, isn't it?' she said, bending to pat the animal. To her surprise it recoiled, snarling. The woman reprimanded it sharply.

'Stop it, Archimedes! There's nothing to growl at.'

'Oh, don't worry, Mrs Skinner,' Vera reassured her. 'I'm sure Archimedes and I will soon be firm friends when we get to know each other.' But her neighbour hurried the little dog along, dragging it like a small toy, and no more was said.

At her own gate Vera encountered the daughter from the

basement flat, a cheerful garrulous girl, still at the local comprehensive school.

'Hullo, Tracey,' she greeted her. 'Did you know Mrs Skinner has a new puppy?' The girl looked at her blankly. Obviously she knew nothing about it. Here was a heaven-sent opportunity for conversation. She looked about her as usual. At that time of day, with any luck, someone else would soon be passing and would hear them talking together. 'She calls it Archimedes. Such a ridiculously long name for such a very small dog. Still, perhaps it's what they call a kennel name. Or maybe he keeps jumping out of his bath . . .' she gabbled on desperately, still getting no response. Tracey had started to walk away. How peculiar; but perhaps she was late for something important.

Vera shrugged off the apparent snub and continued up the path to the front door, her heart sinking a little at the thought of returning once more to her empty room. Then she heard a step behind her and noticed that the window-cleaner had just propped his bicycle against the kerb and was approaching with his bucket and leather. She was quick to respond.

'Oh, you want some clean water. Give me the pail and I'll fill it while you get your ladder.' She held out her hand for the bucket, but he ignored her and continued up the path. After a life-time of snubs, this second rebuff did not offend or surprise her much. She was merely a little puzzled and thought that perhaps he had misunderstood or misheard her. She followed him to the door and waited as he rang the bell for Tracey's mother. It was not worth bothering to get out her own key. In a moment the door was opened and they were confronted with the vision of Mrs Morris, plastic-aproned, tin-opener in one hand, transistor in the other. She juggled to take the bucket and dropped the tin-opener. The window-cleaner and Vera bent simultaneously to pick it up and nearly bumped heads. She laughed, but there was no answering mirth from the man or from Mrs Morris either. 'Oh well, I'll leave you to it,' she said and walked upstairs, feeling again a little abashed.

Once inside her flat, she made for the bedroom, pulled off her coat and turned to the dressing-table to tidy herself. She peered and crouched, but could get no reflection. The looking-glass must have tilted. Irritated, she turned to the wardrobe and opened it to reveal the full-length mirror within. Again

she could not see herself. She swung the door, manoeuvred
from side to side. There was no defect in the glass. The angle of
the room was clearly reflected, even to the other mirror on the
dressing-table. She stood between them, but they continued
emptily to reflect each other in endless decreasing images.
Why did her body not deflect the light?

While she was still puzzling over this, there was a tiny thud
at the window. She ran over and pulled back the curtain. The
cleaner had placed his ladder against the sill and was climbing
with his usual deliberation. A thought occurred to her and she
remained looking out until he rose to her level and their eyes
met. She smiled and mouthed wordlessly at him. He slapped
the dripping leather across the pane, ignoring her totally.
Daring, she made a grimace, but he disregarded this too. Just
then there was a small commotion below. She peered past the
window-cleaner and saw a policeman talking to Mrs Morris.
The window-cleaner descended his ladder and at the same
moment Tracey and the neighbour with the new puppy
arrived from opposite directions. Soon all four were talking
and gesticulating excitedly. The conviction was borne in upon
her that she herself was the subject of their conversation. She
ran from the flat and hurried downstairs. She had a theory to
test and this was the opportunity.

They had all moved to the gate and were talking there.
No-one looked up or moved aside as she approached. Only
Archimedes reacted with a tiny growl. As she walked past
them, un-noticed, it was as if ice-cubes dissolved within her
heart, chilling the blood within her veins. Fear, very deadly
fear, possessed her in that moment. To be dead – for she had no
doubt now that her accident had in fact been fatal – this was
something strange and terrifying. But as she continued unseen
down the busy street, she realized that the change was not so
great as she had imagined. To be unheard, unseen, unrecognized, to seem to have no physical effect on others; these
experiences were not new to her. Her image of herself had
always depended on its reflection back from the reactions of
others and this had been nebulous at best. Suddenly she
experienced a quick surge of joy; she realized that at last she
had found her true vocation. Her whole life had been one of
near invisibility; but she had an inestimable advantage over all
the bewildered dead whom she now saw hammering unheard

at nearby doors, passing bemused through stout pedestrians, hovering pathetically about their former doors. She was accustomed to the status of non-person. She had a life-time of practice behind her. While others were born to a career, she had died to achieve hers, and it would be her supreme happiness and success. Elated now, she floated through the crowds, ready to haunt the living; a perfectly qualified new ghost.

The Chance of a Lifetime

Tom Strachan

I visit the world when I have to. I wear a bright red dress to match my face. Children point, stare, eyes like bubbles on the point of bursting. Their mothers quickly tug them away before anything unpleasant is said. I live in a world where nothing unpleasant must ever be said. I doubt if I'll ever have a child of my own.

Dr Grossman suggested electrotherapy, cosmetics. He was surprised when I turned the idea down.

'It's too late for anything like that,' I told him.

I felt like asking if a nose-job would make him any less of a Jew, but that would've been the bad half of my face talking and I try not to talk with that.

The stain, an ugly maroon blotch, begins quietly by the left eye, curls inward to the nose and down, ending with a neat tuck under the chin. The other side of my face is almost beautiful. I live my life in profile as much as possible.

Nobody seems to know quite why such disfigurements are caused. I imagine that over the years a poisonous sediment settled in my mother's womb: I came into being and lay there dreaming in my nerveless way – and it ate into my face like an acid. Two years later, when my pretty sister Louise was conceived, she had a clean environment to develop in. Lucky Louise.

My mother tells her friends: 'Mary's the brains of the family . . . she's at college now.'

And the friends are all sympathetic smiles, twisting fingers,

nodding heads. Their eyes have a curious habit of landing on
my face and immediately darting back into the air, circling
there, mindless as flies.

It was Louise who suggested the holiday.

'Just you and me,' she said enthusiastically.

The original idea was a fortnight in France. A shortage
of money forced us to change our plans. A fortnight in
Aberystwyth didn't seem quite so exciting.

We stayed in a small hotel which was advertised as being 'on
the front' but, in reality, was halfway up a narrow backstreet,
the sea only visible obliquely between the more expensive
hotels. We were given adjacent rooms with a shared view of
the supermarket opposite.

'It's all a bit posh,' Louise said.

For the first two days it rained most of the time and apart
from one brave venture along the promenade to look at the
pier, we stayed indoors, watching TV in the lounge, drinking
absurdly-named cocktails in the bar. The barman looked like
Dylan Thomas.

The third day, Wednesday, was sunny. We went down to
the beach about ten, stripped to our swimming costumes and
sunbathed. I spread a newspaper over my face.

'I hate the sun in my eyes,' I told Louise.

After an hour or so I was nearly asleep. Louise suddenly
whispered, 'There's two boys over there. They keep looking
at us.'

'Probably fancy a read of the paper,' I said.

Whenever my sister mentions the opposite sex, her
voice develops a sickening tremble. She insists on calling
any male under forty a 'boy'. No doubt she was encour-
aging them, looking without looking, bulging eyes and
puppyfat. A few minutes later she hissed, 'They're coming
over.'

I stayed under my newspaper.

They were soldiers on leave from Ireland. The one called
Terry did all the talking. The other one, Giles, coughed now
and then, and when he thought it was appropriate, sniggered. I
could just imagine him – cauliflower ears, acne, wondering
what to do with his hands.

Terry suggested a ride on the cliff railway.

'We don't even know you,' Louise simpered.

'It's the chance of a lifetime,' Terry said.

I slipped out from under the newspaper and grinned my widest grin. 'What are we waiting for?'

Just for a second they both looked horrified. I imagined them, still wearing swimming trunks and the same stunned expressions, manning a security gate in Belfast.

Terry bought the tickets.

The 'train' was a string of brightly-painted wooden boxes on wheels that were hauled up a rusty track by a winch. Each box had space for two people.

'Doesn't look very safe to me,' Louise said.

Terry took her by the arm. 'Don't worry,' he said, 'the British army's looking after you. What more could anyone ask for?'

He led Louise to the yellow box at the far end of the platform. Giles and I sat side by side, two inches between us, in the lime-green box at the back.

'Should be a good view,' he said.

'I expect that's why they built the railway in the first place,' I said.

He peered over the side at the track and then sat up again, stiff, staring straight ahead. He couldn't even glance at me. He was obviously very worried about something.

The boxes jerked into action and slowly creaked and grated their way to the top. Cardigan Bay was a hazy blue curve below us.

'The people look very small,' Giles said, turning my way briefly and then hastily back at the view.

'They do from a distance,' I told him.

There was a café. We all drank Cokes. Louise and Terry played frantic pinball. Giles and I sat either side of a grimy table. I lit a cigarette. We stared through the small window at the sea.

'We've got to go back on Friday,' he said.

We talked about Ireland. He didn't have anything very interesting to say. I asked him if he liked being a soldier.

'It's a job,' he said.

'So's being a hangman.'

'That's different.'

We all walked along the cliff path towards Borth – Giles and I striding out in front, Terry and Louise hanging back. Louise

was having a giggling fit behind us: something was obviously
very funny.

We got within sight of Borth, but then Louise complained
that her feet were hurting (she was wearing high heels) and we
had to turn back. We returned slowly in a bunch, Louise
hobbling, Terry telling bad jokes. At one point we discussed
the 'world situation'.

Giles said, 'Nuclear missiles are terrible things.'

And Terry laughed. 'At least if there is a Third World War
it'll solve the unemployment problem.'

And then Louise told everyone that wars are silly and if only
all the countries would get rid of their armies, there wouldn't
be any wars at all.

'She's trying to put us out of a job,' Terry said.

He began to tell us about a film he was shown during
training. 'It was all about Vietnam. Jungle warfare. Napalm,'
he said. 'You should see what a mess that stuff makes of your
face . . .'

There was an embarrassed silence (red faces all round) and
then Louise started moaning about her feet again.

'I thought it was going to be a proper path,' she said.

We took the 'train' back down the cliff and then walked
along the promenade to the King's Amusement Arcade, a
large basement hall full of bright lights and whirring
machines. Louise persuaded Terry to play bingo. Giles swaggered up to the rifle-range, rolled up his sleeves, shot six tin
cowboys out of ten, and failed to win a prize.

'Just as well they weren't in the IRA,' I said.

He seemed upset. 'The sights were crooked. It's not my
fault . . . a marksman's only as good as his gun.'

Louise won a pink and white teddybear at the bingo.

Just before opening time we left the arcade and went in
search of a pub. Louise gave her teddybear (already named
Mountbatten – Terry's suggestion) to the first child she came
to – a little girl, chin smeared with green ice cream, watery
eyes.

'I knew she was a generous lady,' Terry said, slipping an
arm around Louise's shoulders.

She didn't resist. 'I'd have felt stupid carrying that around
everywhere,' she said and giggled.

We walked away from the sea, uphill, through the univer-

sity grounds, and came to a small pub that was just opening.
Terry and Giles drank bitter. Louise had a snowball. I had gin
and lemon.

'Gin makes people miserable,' Giles said.

I told him it was his job to keep me happy.

There was a sign hanging over the bar advertising 'Delicious
Hot Meals' and so we all ordered Welsh rarebit, two slices
each. Louise chose the same record on the jukebox three times
running. Near the end of his second pint, Giles showed me a
photograph of his parents. They were standing side by side in
the shadow of a large, curiously-buckled tree. The mother was
immense, her bare arms folded like thick coils of insipid,
mottled meat. The father seemed sadly withered, the pinched
face of a weasel with horribly dilated eyes. It was obviously
one of those marriages in which the wife grows fatter and
fatter and the husband steadily atrophies, as if in the small
hours, entwined in the conjugal bed, some mysterious trans-
ference of flesh takes place.

Halfway through his third pint, Giles told me that his father
had died two years previously (stomach cancer) and now his
mother was involved with a scoutmaster called Rodney.

'That was half the reason I joined up,' he said.

We all left just after ten. We walked back down towards the
sea. It was almost dark. Louise and Terry went for a stumbling
walk along the beach. Giles lurched unsteadily to one of the
promenade benches. I sat beside him. We stared at the last
streaks of the sunset.

'It's beautiful,' he mumbled.

'Everything's beautiful when you're pissed.'

'Not always,' he said. 'And anyway . . . I'm not all that
pissed.'

He put a hand on my knee. It lay there like an inert reptile. I
imagined it suddenly wrenching free from the wrist, leaping
down to the shingle, scuttling to the sea.

'How far is it to your hotel?'

The reptile twitched.

'You'll have to go up the fire-escape,' I said.

It was only a short walk along the corridor from the
fire-escape door to my room. He crept in like a burglar.

'We're trained to be silent,' he hissed.

We sat on the edge of the bed and he kissed me – a tentative,

carefully-placed kiss with eyes closed. I wondered whether his eyes were closed to intensify the tenderness of the moment, or because he couldn't stand looking at my face.

'Shall I turn out the light?' I asked him.

We undressed in the orange glow of the streetlamp outside. The bed was uncomfortably narrow. He smothered the good half of my face with damp kisses. The reptile made an energetic reappearance. There were long moments of sweat and tension. And then nothing: it was like trying to thread a needle with a sliver of jelly.

Suddenly he pulled away, slid out of bed, staggered to the sink. He was violently sick.

'Pity you haven't been trained to puke silently,' I said.

'I think I must've drunk too much,' he groaned, getting back into bed.

A few minutes later he was asleep, mouth hanging open, snoring. I lay awake for most of the night. I heard Louise sneaking in about two, whispering with Terry in the corridor, giggles through the wall. Some time after that, I dozed off for a while and dreamt that a huge man wearing a protective steel helmet was methodically kissing the stained part of my face, surgical kisses that removed the puckered skin, shred by shred, revealing perfect whiteness underneath.

I nudged Giles awake about six-thirty and told him he ought to leave before the hotel got too busy.

'Don't want to damage my reputation,' I said.

He dressed in a hurry, not looking at me.

'See you later,' he said. 'How about midday outside the arcade?'

'Okay,' I said.

But I knew he wouldn't be there. He'd be with Terry in a pub somewhere, huddled in a corner with their manly confidences. And drunk and smug, the coarse remarks: 'Better than a milkbottle' or 'They're all the same with a bag over their heads' – all those sad jokes that men enjoy when they're pretending to be happy.

Digging for Gold

Nicholas Burbridge

M cHale is white, shaking. At the other window his son is drumming his hands on his thighs, pretending to be absorbed in the rhythms of a reel. Wedged between them, the only sister who has chosen to come to the cemetery dabs her eyes with a wet handkerchief. In front there are two young cousins dressed in black leather, with bright shocks of hair and clusters of metal rings. The seat next to the driver remains empty until shortly before they drive off, when the door opens and Uncle Barney pokes his head in to ask if there is room for one more.

As soon as he gets in he starts talking, lighting a cigarette and offering the packet round. The long sleek black car quickly fills with smoke. Dominic, whose funeral it is, lies in a new coffin a few yards ahead. There are two official vehicles and a small posse of second-hand cars and motorbikes. One of the cousins asks if anyone minded her putting a small candle in a glass jar on the coffin while communion was being taken. No one appears to have noticed. Uncle Barney, who has paused momentarily, takes up again where he left off, leaning over the back of the seat, cigarette in hand. Meanwhile the driver calculates what attitude he should take towards his passengers. He decides two things. First, they are Irish. Second, his task is simply to take them to the cemetery and bring them back. He allows himself a sideward glance at Uncle Barney. The other cousin sneers at his back as he steers into the main thoroughfare.

Uncle Barney flicks his ash into the ashtray indifferently. 'Aye, you wouldn't believe it but the friggin' car ran out of

petrol just outside town. Couldn't find a garage at all. Had to call the AA. Sure, I'm late for a funeral, says I. Jeez, I never thought the day'd come.'

There is a brief silence while they draw on their cigarettes. Every hand is trembling.

'An', sure, it's hardly a year since Granny Deirdre went an' fell downstairs. Do you remember that one, Peter?'

McHale nods two or three times, unable to control his facial muscles. 'Aye, we went back together on the shuttle.'

'It was a fine funeral. Not a duncher to be seen.' Uncle Barney lowers his voice. 'You know, I stayed on with the oul' folks after. An' you know wee Joan, like she's wasted away so much she's all skin an' bone, an' what with bein' an oul' spinster an' all she's never had much crack in her anyway. Well, there we all was sittin' in the parlour mullin' things over, an' someone says, "Sure, I wonder who'll be next to go" – not meanin' nothin' at all. An', sure, everyone turns an' looks at wee Joan, sittin' in the corner knittin' away, an' not a word's said. Jeez, I had to leave the room to stop pissin' meself.'

Everyone in the car is grinning as they halt at a traffic light. A number of pedestrians peer in at the window. The driver looks affronted. They move off again.

Uncle Barney strokes his long red nose. In him the family lineaments have not diminished over the years, while his brother seems to have grown old too quickly, with his blurred beaten expression under a few wisps of white hair. 'It's good to get together anyhow. I hardly see yous all from one year to the next.'

McHale has now stopped shivering and decides to chance a joke himself. 'Aye, an' we're disappearin' fast, man.'

While the others laugh his daughter begins weeping. Uncle Barney looks out of the window. McHale, who hid his own sorrow at the church by holding the women to his breast and shedding his tears in their hair, immediately consoles her. All the women in the family have long thick hair. It was said before and after the service; it will be repeated at the cemetery and in the church hall: the McHales are a handsome breed. The girl wiping her eyes will later grow so tired of strangers' comments she will retort that Dominic will not be looking so handsome in a few weeks' time, and succeed in offending the nervous new curate who swung the censer over her brother's

coffin. She will ask to be forgiven. He will oblige. It is his trade.

'Ah well,' says Uncle Barney, 'if you don't laugh you cry. There's not a truer word been said. Sure, you'd think with comin' over here we'd leave the trouble behind us.'

'Aye, but you can't just run away –' Sean immediately wishes he had not spoken, but the reel in his head is gone now.

Uncle Barney agrees with him. 'So how far is it now anyway?'

'Up on the hill there, Barney.' McHale is relieved that the inevitable inquest has been postponed.

'I see where you mean.' Uncle Barney points. 'We'll not be long there. It's too cold for a priest to hang about with no cacks on.'

There are several hold-ups at junctions and crossings on local roads familiar to those hemmed in in the funeral cars. In time to come they will remember, as they walk the streets, how they drove in this bleak convoy. From almost any point en route to the cemetery the block of flats called Carson House is visible. It is not difficult to imagine a tiny figure on a tenth floor balcony tipping himself off. Such is the geography of the suburbs.

When the car reaches the cemetery gates Uncle Barney stops talking to light another cigarette. Sean is surprised that funeral cars are equipped with electric lighters. He tries hard to listen to his uncle but they are already driving sedately among the headstones. He looks round at the others to see if they too might be imagining the burial ahead. As they draw up at the spot he begins to feel sick. There is nowhere to run. A mass of grey stones stretches as far as he can see.

At the grave Dominic's coffin is waiting on a swathe of artificial grass. Uncle Barney stands by his brother as the last of the dead boy's punk friends arrive and gather desultorily. 'Jeez, I hate these places at the best of times, but with this lot here you'd think we were in hell itself.'

McHale is not listening now. The warmth of the car, filled with cigarette smoke and the distraction of travelling, has disappeared. He is looking into the grave. He cannot believe what is about to happen.

'Och, come on now, Peter. It's soon over, I tell you.'

McHale nods without looking up. He is grateful for his

brother's arm. Beside him his two children also support one
another. The coffin remains on the green in front of them.

The priest arrives, waddling with the curate in tow towards
the small circle of ill-fitting suits and Mohican haircuts. The
driver of the car stands with his associates at one side, wondering if they have made similar calculations to his own. As they
cluster in the frost, the gravedigger waits conspicuously apart,
leaning on his spade, watching sardonically. Uncle Barney is,
at last, quiet.

Dominic is lowered into his hole after a brief prayer.
McHale, his son and daughter, take the small plastic pistol
in turn and squirt a jet of holy water onto the sheathed
box. There is a muttered 'Amen'. Flowers are thrown into
the grave. It is bitterly cold on the bare hill. The peeling off
begins.

On the way back to the church hall Uncle Barney has his
place in the front seat, but the young cousins have joined their
friends in another car. As they pull away from the scene one or
two of the punks are still pulling flowers from wreaths to
throw onto the coffin.

Uncle Barney says, 'So what's all this about Siobhan gettin'
hitched to a Brit?'

The slow thaw starts again. He empties his cigarette packet.
McHale once more finds himself drawn into conversation. His
children also seem keen to talk now. By the time they are
driving directly towards Carson House, towering against the
blue winter sky, they are laughing again. The driver is thinking he will soon be rid of them.

McHale decided that the doors must be locked. He scurried to
the back of the hall. Meanwhile others arrived and shivered on
the steps. Uncle Barney tried the doors himself. The catch was
stiff. He pulled them open. McHale appeared in silhouette,
muttering apologies, then hurried off to the toilet where he
stayed until he had vomited his breakfast.

The hall was twenty foot square, crossed by two trestles
surrounded by wooden chairs. Plates of meat and cheese,
salads and mince pies had been laid out by the women who had
avoided going to the cemetery. By the time McHale emerged,
the mourners had installed themselves in small groups. He
paused in the corridor, looking at the half of the hall he could

see, bathed in weak sunlight. Then he stepped into the priest's
genial embrace.

'God bless you, Peter. It was a truly moving ceremony. I'm
grateful to you and your family.'

Uncle Barney was talking at Dominic's other sisters.
McHale looked for his wife. She was sitting huddled over a
portable oil heater, long red hair falling over her shoulders,
dark glasses ringing her cheekbones, thin and white. She was
also laughing. The curate had said something to her about the
consolation man and wife could find in one another at such a
time. McHale crossed to her and held her hand. She let him,
but did not respond.

'You're evil. Leave me alone.'

Mary McHale had made sure the whole family were aware
that these were her son's last words, as he struggled free from
her and plunged to the ground, where he lay, for some
minutes, still alive, in a limp crucifix. She had run down ten
floors of acrid-smelling stone stairs to find two strangers
standing over his body, while his black eyes turned slowly one
way and another. Behind the dark glasses she had worn ever
since she could see nothing else.

McHale smiled invisibly. He decided that the only thing
was to get drunk.

Someone had given Sean a tin whistle. He piped a few
aimless notes, then the reel which had been thrumming in his
head echoed through the hall in shrill metallic notes. The tune
was known to all the family. The priest clapped his hands
vigorously as if in blessing. When the reel ended everyone applauded. Then there was a shout of, 'Barney, give
us a wee song, go on now.' Uncle Barney declined – he
was on only his third Jameson. Sean began a slow air on the
whistle.

The new curate did not share his superior's enthusiasm. It
was an English parish after all . . . He said as much, to one of
Dominic's schoolteachers. As soon as he had spoken he wondered if he would appear uncharitable. The tall bearded man
beside him merely muttered that he liked the music. Forgiveness was not his trade. The curate then rekindled his sense of
impropriety, looking from the corner of his eye at the be-
reaved mother, reflecting how crone-like she appeared. His
studious face was marked with indifference.

Uncle Barney was eventually persuaded to sing. The piercing tones of the whistle were replaced by his mellifluous tenor voice.

> *Oh Mary this London's a wonderful sight*
> *With people here working by day and by night*
> *They don't sow potatoes not barley nor wheat*
> *But there's gangs of them diggin' for gold in the street*
> *At least when I asked them that's what I was told*
> *So I just took a hand at this diggin' for gold*
> *But for all that I found there I might as well be*
> *Where the mountains of Mourne sweep down to the sea*

The family sat in silence, afraid to glance at one another, as he stood singing with his eyes closed, and his hands thrust deep into his jacket pockets; but then, when he held up one finger and wagged it to and fro in time, voice by voice they joined in with him, until they were all singing together.

After the last verse came to an end McHale suddenly felt an urge to eat. He covered a plate with cold food but he could only manage a couple of mouthfuls. He filled his glass and drank instead. As he stared down at the floor absently, he found he was looking into Dominic's grave. The digger was shovelling earth over the coffin. It had all but disappeared. He began shivering again. Uncle Barney was there once more to take his arm.

He whispered, 'Peter, you have the devil by the tail, an' that's the truth.'

Those least involved began to wonder if anything else should happen; they were growing anxious to escape the hall. For their part, the punks, who had spent their time flicking food at each other, were planning the evening's entertainment, aware that Dominic would not be among them. The family began to separate, uncertainly.

Uncle Barney consulted his watch and realized that the pubs were still open for another hour at least. He had done what he had come to. He looked for his brother who had wandered away. McHale was standing again by his wife, who seemed to be falling asleep over the heater. He was running a hand through his wisps of white hair, looking vaguely around him, as if he had glimpsed the hall as it might have been if it were

someone else's wake: the food on the tables, the strangers, the huddles of chairs.

'Peter, Peter, now which of your handsome daughters is it who wants to see me about a wedding?' The priest had come invisibly to his side.

McHale tried to collect himself, as he saw Uncle Barney leaving by the back door with a gesture to imply that he would meet him later at home. 'Ah well,' he said, 'that's Siobhan, Father. The tall girl with the long black hair. She wants to wait till all this is blown over but she'd like to have a wee word all the same.'

The priest beamed. 'I'm very glad, Peter, very glad. A marriage in the family will make all the difference. As I said in church, we must always be prepared to begin again.' He paused then added in a whisper, 'It is people like you, Peter, who give meaning to my vocation.'

As he crossed the room, his vestment rustling, McHale vaguely remembered his sermon – something about dark days of winter, the promise of buds on trees, flowers in the spring to come. Spoken from the pulpit it had seemed to have a meaning. He watched the priest take his daughter's hand and nod vigorously as she introduced him to the nondescript young man who was to become her husband, without any sense of pleasure. It was another man's son.

Life in the Sun
A Modern Fable

Clare West

For a week after her arrival, Sarah Gunn felt ill, and lay in her room in the rented villa on the orange-farm, sweating in the heat, pressed in on by the shuttered darkness. She could not explain her strange queasiness. Was it the heat? Or the unvarying meat dishes in oily tomato sauce? Or the evening timetable she had to work? Or was it the men? Men everywhere, in blue pyjamas, in long striped nightshirts, in elegant Italian suits, in workman's overalls, in smart white uniforms, following, pushing, pinching, feeling, leering, whispering 'You come bed me?' in between clicking their teeth, picking their noses, clearing their throats and spitting, scratching and continually adjusting their genitals between their legs. There were hardly any women. They scurried in and out of each other's flats, or blindly across the road to the market, completely swathed in white garments, held closely over the head and face to obscure all except one kohl-rimmed eye, a menace to traffic but more or less expendable.

Gradually she grew accustomed to it, and began to study her new surroundings. She started learning Arabic, the Libyan dialect, so that she could communicate with the people on their own terms. With other teachers she made trips East to Benghazi, the Green Mountains and the ancient Greek ruins of Cyrene. They drove South on a hazardous pot-holed road to the desert with its prehistoric cave-drawings, and to Sebha, near the Chad border. She delighted in the welcome they received from villagers, who lived up to the highest standards of Arab hospitality in offering the strangers warm Pepsi, cold couscous, mint tea, and thick sweet coffee, which left her

mouth full of grounds. She loved the natural way of living, without all the enfeebling mod cons of European life. She rather shuddered in the butcher's, where you identified the meat available from the dripping severed head outside the door and pointed to the part of the carcase that you wanted. But she approved of buying eggs covered in hen-droppings – it proved they were free-range – and even enjoyed cooking with a Calor Gas bottle, which you changed when empty at a garage. There were often shortages, gas, sugar or tinned tomatoes. When the banana-boat came in, everybody ate them constantly for a fortnight, frantically swopping recipes for banana-cakes and pancakes, then there would be none for a month. There were no drains, so when it rained, which it did very heavily twice a year for three days at a time, all the main streets were flooded. Libyans found these conditions so novel and fascinating that as soon as it started to rain they all jumped in their cars and drove round town stalling and jamming the streets. She had informative chats with other expats in the Tuesday afternoon queue for the *Sunday Times* outside the main newsagent's. She noted down all these peculiarities in her notebook, and described them to her friends in long letters.

When she met an Algerian at a barbecue arranged by the teachers, she was charmed by his European sophistication. They talked and laughed for hours at a time in French. She felt her accent was improving a lot. They made love. She was a little disappointed. It didn't seem the sort of experience to inspire the world's greatest writers. Still, you probably had to improve your technique at that just like anything else. She determined to buy the Karma Sutra when back in England on holiday, to study the positions (it would never get through Customs if she ordered it here). He moved into the villa she had been sharing with two other teachers, who eventually felt *de trop* and moved out. When he asked her to marry him, she was thrilled. A whole new book fell open before her. He would explain to her the spiritual intricacies of Islam. She would go on a diet and lose weight: he didn't mind about her grey hair. They would travel a lot: he would show her the sights of all the Arab capitals. They might settle in a neutral country like French Canada. With his help she would be able to plunge much deeper into understanding the complex layers of Arab culture. She agreed, despite the objections of her

family, who didn't realize how it would enlarge her horizons.

In the first two years she felt she was making great progress. She became almost bilingual in French. She met his large family, was warmly greeted and learnt from his younger sisters how to make couscous, the weekly Friday lunch, and shorba, the mutton soup used to take the edge off the appetite when breaking fast in Ramadan: she noted down carefully the quantities and the spices. She was running the villa single-handed (he was out a lot), acquiring new skills daily. She learnt to swab the Italian stone floors, bent double like the Arab women, moving slowly backwards, pulling the damp floor-cloth towards her in a sweeping movement, and to check the shine by looking back along the floor against the light. Her dictionaries, diaries, reference books and notebooks were labelled and stacked in order above her desk. Juggling teaching and housework meant a tight schedule which she kept to rigidly, as being five minutes late back from the market reduced her cooking time: she had to prepare fresh meat and vegetables because he didn't approve of convenience foods. She agreed: she was happy to learn to cook the proper way, not out of packets. She gardened: she sowed lawn seed she found in a grocer's in Shara Istiklal, sold as bird seed, and cut the whole area on her hands and knees with a pair of shears, her hands trembling all that evening: she planted rose-bushes and vegetables. They made love quite often: it didn't get any more exciting for her, but he seemed pleased with her so she felt she must be doing all the right things. She was buoyed up by the originality of her position, by the fact of her marriage, by the wealth she still had to discover, by the constant cleansing sun.

There was an intermediate phase when she began to won-der. She found herself saying doubtfully, 'After all, it's better being married than an old maid, isn't it?' She lied to her mother in her letters that everything was still marvellous. She discov-ered that he didn't always tell the truth, had a vicious temper, and sulked for days on end. She came to the end of her recipe notebook and decided not to start a new one: it hardly seemed worth it, as he didn't find her attempts successful, always adding an extra heap of salt and his own harisa, the hot red pepper paste. She defended him to her friends, but only cried into the breakfast washing-up, sobbing to the rainbow bub-

bles, when he stamped out of the house after an argument.
They always made it up, but these days she didn't seem to be
learning anything, in fact she was so confused she felt gaps in
her memory and a stone weighting down her chest.

One day it happened quite suddenly. She was walking
through the soft sand between the orange-trees, avoiding the
fallen, mouldy ones. She'd just seen him off to work. It was
December and the trees were loaded. He'd called her a slut
because she'd left the evening's washing-up. She'd been a bit
surprised herself. The kitchen had stacks of used plates piled
up now. She came to her favourite, the grapefruit, with its
huge pale yellow globes and luscious pink insides. She passed
the Seville oranges, which she alone picked, for marmalade, as
the farmer hated the bitter taste and distorted skin. It was
getting hot as the sun dappled the sand through the leaves. The
strength of the colours, blue, green, yellow, orange, attacked
her. She came out of the shade into a brilliant clearing. White
zigzags caught at her eyelids. She had wasted four years on
him! He was violent and dishonest. He did up rotten cars in his
spare time and sold them at a profit to foreigners. He was
jealous and knew nothing of Arab culture. He couldn't speak
or write Arabic correctly. He even spoke French ungrammati-
cally. She was picking up his mistakes and unmistakable
accent. He was becoming more of a fanatic about Islam,
obliging her to fast for the whole month of Ramadan, to study
the Koran, and to abstain from alcohol and pork. She had to
get away. She needed her friends. She hated the alien sun.

It was as she was at her desk that evening after supper,
sorting out her papers, checking her passport, that he came
with his quick, quiet step into the room. She turned and asked
him, her voice unvarying in pitch, if she could leave. Although
she knew him by now, she still expected a rational, polite
exchange of views. She wasn't prepared for his rage, which
knocked her off the chair and brought down the book-case
above the desk, scattering her beloved books over the polished
tiles. He dived for her address-book and ripped it into fluttering fragments, his face twisted and grinning. 'You need a
husband's permission for an exit visa, don't forget.'

The mosquito-door on the veranda banged behind him. She
heard the sewing-machine noise of the 2-chevaux start up and
whirr away. He'd taken her car and her passport. She carefully

put back all the books. She sat for a long time at the kitchen table, listening to the call to prayer resounding on the evening air from the mosque nearby. 'Allah hu' Akbar.' God is great. She tried hard to glue the pieces of paper together, poring shortsightedly over them. It was still very hot. The back door was open. The bougainvillea's harsh purple sprawled over the white garden wall. From where she sat she could see a huge red furry caterpillar demolishing the last of her hibiscus leaves. Scraps of unintelligible Arabic floated to her from the Egyptian farm-workers going down the track. The pieces wouldn't fit. She shivered in the heat.

The Wedding Jug

Philip Smith

I stood at the back door and looked up at the moon. Its brightness from over the dark hump of the hillside made clear the pale drifting smoke from somebody's garden. The woodsmoke and the moon made me restless, eager to be moving in the sharp October night.

I had been standing on the door step for several minutes, staring, wondering how on earth I was going to get through the evening. Saturday. Saturday night and I was stuck with my grandmother.

The others had gone – my mother and my sister, both courting. Neither of them seemed to care about my grandmother. Nothing much was ever said, they just went out, leaving her alone, or most often with me to sit at home because I just could not see that she should be left on her own on a Saturday night, with no one to talk to and everybody else out at the pictures or dancing.

Of course, I would have gone if I had been able to get away first. Then I would not have had to think about the old woman, plodding about the routines that she would fill her evening with. I would have slipped away and left my mother and Ena to argue, not with each other but with my grandmother, each separately conducting a running battle as they prepared for the night out. One of them would lose and the loser would stay at home, angry and frustrated at being in on a Saturday night, the one night of all the week for pleasure. Well, anticipation of pleasure. There was hardly ever any real fulfilment of hopes but at least the ritual of going out to the Queen's Ballroom or the Plaza or the Regal

brought with it a possibility and that was something to fight for.

'Where are *you* going?' my grandmother would demand of her daughter, forty-six and a widow for fifteen years.

'I'm going out.' My mother's reply would be even and she would look defiance as I imagine she had done at sixteen, and always would do.

'You're not going with that man are you?'

'What do you mean "that man"? You know who I'm going with and you know his name.'

'You should be ashamed of yourself, a woman of your age.' She was ready for a long session of baiting.

'I'm not a girl and I know what I'm doing. I deserve a bit of pleasure and I'm going to take it while I can. Damn it I've been at it all week skivvying, and you sit there like a queen, waiting for Annie to come in, and Annie to get your food, and Annie to do this and Annie to do that.'

'A queen? Sitting on my own in this house all night and nobody to say a word to? You don't care about anybody but yourself.'

And so it would go on until my mother would explode in a rage of swearing and tears and storm out through the front gate, running down to the corner of the street where Sid would be waiting.

Sometimes it would be my sister's preparations that my grandmother would notice first. Ena would be combing her hair and putting her lipstick on in front of the mirror over the living room fireplace.

The old woman would have washed up the Saturday tea things and Ena would have wiped and they would have chatted quite happily as on any other weekday, but then she would be aware of the girl having slipped away while she was still emptying the bowl and wiping the draining board. She would notice Ena's quick, excited movements as she snapped her powder compact shut, and put it with her comb and lipstick into her handbag.

'You're not leaving me on my own are you?'

'It's all right, Gran, I'm only going to the pictures.'

'What time will you be back?'

'Oh I won't be long. I'll be back just after ten.'

'But what am *I* going to do? Here on my own.'

'Why don't you put the wireless on? And do some knitting. You'll be all right.'

'What – and me here on my own like some lost thing? I'm not staying here. I'm going. I don't know why I ever gave my home up, but I'll find somewhere. You'll see, I'll find somewhere. I'm not living like this any more. A dog wouldn't be treated like this.'

She would start taking her pinafore off – her sign to one and all that she was going to get her hat and coat.

At this point I would melt.

'It's all right, Gran. I'll be in. I'm not doing anything tonight. I'm going to be in.'

My sister would have slipped away. As far as I knew both she and my mother would spend their evening without a care. I was with the old woman, and if I were not, then she would still be all right. Nothing was going to happen to her. She'd be in bed when they got home and in the morning there would be Sunday dinner to prepare and that would make it easier to shut off from the complaining.

It was not like that for me, though. I just couldn't go if there was a chance that the old woman would be left alone. Sometimes my sister would decide to have a Saturday night at home if there'd been a tiff with a boyfriend or if her girlfriend had a cold, and I could go off with Ted and Ronnie and the others and feel contented. But, if there was any doubt, the thoughts of my grandmother would cloud my pleasure. In the middle of a film or on the bus home I would want to rush back quickly out of guilt and pity, anxious to find her happy and peaceful, hating the bickering that would last well into Sunday.

But tonight I had no worries about that at least. Whatever it was like, it would be a peaceful evening for both of us: for her, because she had me to talk to, and for me because my conscience would be clear and Sunday, at least, would be calm.

A double-decker bus, filled with people, and bright with yellow light went by between the houses beyond the back gardens. A girl ran past the front gate, her high heels clopping on the pavement. She was followed by another, calling out to her to wait. A dog barked briefly and was answered by another in the distance. Then it became quiet. I turned on the door-step and went into the back-kitchen.

My grandmother was coming out of the living-room.

'I'll put some coal on and then we can have a nice fire.'

'It's OK, Gran. I'll get it.'

She took hold of my arm, her grasp tight and strong, and pushed me out of the way, gently.

'You sit down. Leave the fire to me.'

I knew there would be no winning of that argument. The rituals of building and replenishing fires were part of the rhythm of her life, and not to be disturbed. She would bend her arthritic legs painfully in the gloom of the coal-shed and swing the seven-pound hammer to break the lumps into just the sizes she needed.

I went into the living-room and got my book off the dresser. Thomas Hardy – *The Return of the Native*. I'd heard about Thomas Hardy at school: somebody had said he was as famous as Dickens, so that was good. I had trembled a bit in the library that afternoon when I had stood in front of the section where Hardy was. It was always like that starting a new author, thinking of all the things you never knew, things which were now going to be revealed to you.

I sat down in the 'basket-chair', a wicker chair that someone had given my mother because it had a few woodworm holes. On the other side of the fireplace was our other arm-chair, high-backed, with here and there a small split in the covering and a few horse hairs showing through.

My grandmother put the shovelful of coal down on to the fender and, with a slight grunt, picked up the iron poker and started to stir the fire. The fresh lumps were thrown on and she straightened up, the shovel hanging down by her side, in a faint haze of smoke and coal dust.

'Where's your pipe tonight?' she asked.

'It's over there.'

'Well, have a smoke. I like the smell. It shows there's a man in the house. I used to say that to Edward when he was alive.'

She went out through the back-kitchen to the coal-shed and I heard her throw the shovel down and turn the key in the lock. No more coal would be needed tonight. She shut the back-door and turned the key in the lock.

'Don't lock the door, Gran. Mam and Ena will be coming in.'

She gave no sign of having heard. She was washing her

hands under the tap. It didn't matter: I could unlock it later.
There was plenty of time.

The first small flames were beginning to come through the
layer of small coal, lighting up the grey-brown smoke that was
still thick in the chimney.

As I sat reading I was aware of her movements from the
sounds: the bang of the cupboard-door under the sink as she
got out the paraffin-can and a slight squeak as she unscrewed
the top.

'Oh, that damn lamp! My head will never save my feet.'

I broke off from my book.

'I'll get it, Gran.'

'No, you stay where you are. You sit there. I'll go up and get
it and then I can settle.' She put her hand on my shoulder,
pressed me down, and grinned. I was aware of strength in her
thin, white arm.

When Vivienne was with me I was glad of the times when
my grandmother went upstairs to fetch her lamp. Sometimes
on a Saturday we would both keep her company and would sit
eagerly waiting for the chance to kiss whenever she left the
room. As now, my grandmother would make her way slowly
upstairs, and I would leap out of my chair to the girl, to kiss
her, to squeeze her breasts, as much as possible before the old
woman came back down. I could rely on my grandmother,
though. There would be things to be done up there, even on a
cold winter's night: the lamp-wick would need trimming, the
lamp glass would need to be breathed on and polished,
something she needed for her knitting would have to be
rummaged for in a drawer. And when she did come down, she
would clump extra heavily on the lino of the stairs and give the
loose door-knob a distinct rattle before she came back into the
living-room.

She now walked to her drawer, took out her knitting and sat
down opposite me.

I became absorbed by my reading, and a quietness settled in
the room. The tapping of knitting needles and the occasional
rustle of the now-glowing fire were sounds that touched only
the outer edge of my mind. Occasionally I would look up as I
turned a page, and note my grandmother in that repetitive and
only half-conscious way in which a mother will check a
sleeping child with a single there-and-back motion of the eyes.

She was knitting a scarf, the only thing I had ever known her to knit, a long strip of red, brown, green, yellow, black in sections of random sizes according to the amount of wool she could find or unravel from some previous scarf that none of us could bring ourselves to wear.

I supposed that I would always connect my grandmother with knitting, and cream crackers, and pinafores.

In a little while, about eight-thirty, she would start to prepare her supper: cream-crackers and a cup of Oxo. These and porridge were the only things I had known her eat. 'Damn jockey's food,' she called it. She had long ago lost all her teeth and I could not imagine her with anything other than the sucked-in cheeks of a Mr Punch, and a wrap-round pinafore. We had only one photograph of her, taken in her forties, standing at her cottage gate, in her pinafore, with her sunken cheeks, smiling up at somebody, but old. She had never been other than old to me.

She bent forward now to pick up the poker and one of her needles clattered on to the steel fender.

'I'll do the fire, Gran.'

'No, no. It only needs a bit of a poke. You just pass me the tape-measure out of that jug.'

'Which jug?' I was looking at the shelves of the dresser. There were the Coronation mugs – mine and my sister's for George VI and Edward VIII, my mother's for George V, my grandmother's for Edward VII, and a miscellaneous collection of small vases and jugs and coloured glass dishes.

'That jug there by your hand. Yes, that's it. Give it to me; I'll find it.'

I handed her the glass jug, heavily patterned with embossed squares, and settled back into my chair. The wind seemed to be rising: the draught in the chimney was drawing the fire into a paler, hotter red. I rested both feet on the bars of the iron door of the oven next to the open fire.

'This was my wedding jug,' she said.

'Sorry. What did you say, Gran?'

'It was on the table on my wedding day. Full of rum.'

'Full of rum?' I had never tasted rum, nor even smelt it, but the thought of my grandmother being near a whole jug full of alcohol was deeply surprising.

'Yes, my mother had it filled with rum. We had it on the

table in the village hall, on a big white, starched table cloth. Edward and I – Edward, that was your grandfather – sat at the top end of the table. It was lovely. We had a jug of rum and a jug of sherry and a jug of whisky and a jug of port wine.'

'Did you drink all that?'

'Course we did! It was a hot day. We had a table full of things and a lovely white cloth that my mother had. We had boiled ham and pickled onions and tomatoes and plates of bread and butter, and currant bread and currant cake.'

'Did you have a wedding cake, Gran?'

She seemed not to hear this.

'Do you know – in the middle of all that I saw a little boy standing at the door of the hall. He stood there with his cap in his hand, looking, and then he saw me and came up to where I was sitting. He had been running and he was sweating. I always remember that – he had little drops of sweat across here (she ran a forefinger along her upper lip). He was holding something in his right hand. It was a clean, white handkerchief, folded. He said, "I've brought a present for you," and he gave me the handkerchief. It had something wrapped in it. I took it in my hand like that (she opened her left hand, palm uppermost, and made delicate gestures of unfolding with the thumb and forefinger of her right hand.) and I opened it. Do you know what was in it? A gold watch. Very thin. A very, very thin gold watch. Very delicate. I knew whose it was. It was Tommy's. He was very proud of it. It had belonged to his father – and he'd sent it to me on my wedding day.'

'Who was Tommy?'

'Tommy? He was my lover.'

I had been staring into the fire, grasping every word with my head down. Now I looked up and met my grandmother's eyes. They were calm and, I noticed for the first time, bright blue in the withered skin.

'You see, I had two of them – him and Edward. I had to choose, didn't I? I couldn't go on with the two of them. It had to be the one or the other. I couldn't go on messing about with two.'

I nodded as though I knew, but my stomach trembled at the thought of a woman 'messing about'. My chest was pounding at the picture of a woman with two men – and two men with one woman.

'He was such a tender boy – Tommy – so gentle . . .'
She smiled, as though recalling a child.
'– but – I married your grandfather.'
I tried to make my voice casual with the question.
'Why did you choose Edward, Gran?'
'Who knows?'
I noticed that she had breathed in deeply, and was almost
sighing as the breath came out. There was suddenly a tiredness
about her. 'Who knows?' she said again.

'Anyway – on the day of my wedding Tommy sent me a
present. He sent me his lovely, thin watch. And then – do you
know what he did?'

I could feel my head lowering, and had to lift my chin and
raise my eyes to meet hers. She held my look, as though I were
leaving for a long journey.

Her voice was even and clear. She said:
'He went out into his mother's garden – to the big apple tree
there and then he hanged himself.'

The old woman sat upright, looking now into the darkening glow of the fire, the glass jug cradled in her hands on her
lap.

There was a rustle as the embers settled onto the bottom of
the grate and one or two flecks of ash were carried by the
smoke up into the chimney.

Notes on the Authors

Acknowledgements

NOTES ON THE AUTHORS

F. Bennett is British, a nature and animal lover who worked on the big cattle and sheep stations in the Great Outback of Australia for years, and travelled extensively over that vast country. He is now retired and lives in Hastings.

Margaret Browne was born in Birkenhead, Cheshire. She has had poems published in various magazines and anthologies in this country and abroad. She was a winner of the Radio Kent Play Award and a Mason Hall Award for Creative Writing.

Nicholas Burbridge was born in 1954. He graduated with a first in English from Exeter University and, after extensive travels as a folk musician, settled in Brighton with his wife and son. His work has appeared in leading periodicals, Arts Council anthologies, and on BBC Radio.

Mary Foulkes was born in Shropshire, grew up in London and South Wales, and has lived in Tunbridge Wells with her husband and two sons for the past seventeen years. After having one short story published in a children's magazine nearly forty years ago, she has done no writing until joining the Pantiles Writers' Workshop in February 1983. Since then she has had one story accepted by Radio Kent and is working on several more.

Dorothy Goulden was born in Manchester and settled in Sussex in 1948. She is married with a grown-up family and works as a secretary at the University of Sussex. She loves Brighton and lives in a terraced house in the centre of town. Her main interests in writing are short stories and plays.

Eugenie Hill was born in Lancashire and began writing seriously at the age of six. A number of her stories have been
published in England and overseas and broadcast by the BBC.
Her first novel, *A More Innocent Time*, was a Literary Guild
Selection in America in 1980 and she has since completed two
more novels. Eugenie Hill is married and has lived for the past
ten years in Brighton.

Thomas Hinde lives in Sussex and is married to Susan Chitty,
the biographer. He has been a Visiting Professor of English at
Boston University. He has published sixteen novels including
Mr Nicholas, *The Day The Call Came*, *Our Father* and *Daymare*.
He has also written books on travel, gardening, social history,
and also forest history. He regularly reviews novels for the
Sunday Telegraph.

Kelvin I. Jones was born in 1948 in Bexley, Kent. He is a
teacher who lives in Rochester with his wife, and two cats. His
writings include articles on local history for *Bygone Kent* and
ghost stories (one of which, 'The Green Man', has appeared in
Fantasy Tales). He is the winner of Gravesend's Mason Hall
Literary Award 1984 for an anti-nuclear poem. His main
interest is Sherlock Holmes.

Gabriel Josipovici was born in Nice in 1940. He lived in Egypt
from 1945 to 1956, when he came to this country. At present
Professor of English in the School of European Studies at the
University of Sussex, he is the author of seven novels, two
volumes of short stories, four critical works (one of which,
The Lessons of Modernism, won the South East Arts Literature
Prize in 1978), and of numerous stage and radio plays.

Dick Kempson was born in Essex in 1956. Apart from periods
of travel and study, he was brought up in East Sussex and now
works as a teacher there. *A Walk on the Common* is his first story
to be published, although he has already published poetry.

Francis King, the editor of this collection, was born in Switzer-
land in 1923 and spent his childhood in India. While still an
undergraduate at Balliol College, Oxford, he published three
novels. He continued to write while working for the British
Council in Italy, Greece, Egypt, Finland and Japan. He became a freelance writer in 1965. He is now drama critic of the

Sunday Telegraph and a fortnightly reviewer of novels for the *Spectator*. His most recent novels are *Act of Darkness* and *Voices in an Empty Room*.

Beryl Lewin was born and educated in Surrey, but has lived in Kent since 1959. She trained as a journalist in Cornwall and later worked for the BBC. She has written for radio and revue and in 1984 won the Thanet Poetry Competition and the Tom Busby Memorial Cup for Poetry. She is married to a lawyer and has a grown-up daughter. Her interests include writing, theatre-going, Siamese cats and narrow boats.

Sylvia Monro was bred in the wilds of Cornwall and is one of the Coode family which figures in county annals from the early fourteenth century. Her first love is music and she trained under Sir Steuart Wilson. At the start of the 1939 war she switched to nursing but before peace broke out she married a Gaelic lawyer. After bringing up a family she has had involvement with cricket, ski-ing, boats, horses, also church work, Guides, and a garden, all of which have kept her for many years too busy for much else.

Wendy Perriam was born in London in 1940, read History at St Ann's College, Oxford and now lives in Surrey. She worked as a copywriter in advertising for twelve years, writing poetry and short stories in her spare time. Now she works full time as a novelist and is published by Michael Joseph and Penguin Books. Her novels include *Absinthe for Elevenses*, *Cuckoo*, *After Purple*, *Born of Woman* and a new one due for publication in 1985, entitled *The Stillness the Dancing*.

Jack L. Phillips lives with his wife and son in Dover. He was born in 1934, and attended (with little enthusiasm) various schools in Middlesex, Lincolnshire, Yorkshire and Devon. After a succession of jobs he drifted towards the sea and has been, amongst other things, seaman, pilot-boat coxswain, fisherman and shipwright. Two years ago he took a course in creative writing at the Dover Adult Education Centre and he hopes to publish a novel.

Rosemary Sayers lives in Brighton and is a forty-year-old housewife. Apart from working as a provincial journalist, before the birth of her three children, she has had no previous work published. She meets regularly with a small group of